The
Singing
Serpent

THE SINGING SERPENT

CATHERINE JONES PAYNE

FATHOM INK

FATHOM INK PRESS

The Singing Serpent

Copyright 2022 by Catherine Jones Payne

All rights reserved. Except as permitted under the U.S. Copyright Act of 1976, no part of this publication may be reproduced, stored in a retrieval system, or transmitted in any form or by any means electronic, mechanical, photocopying, recording, or otherwise without the written permission of the author. For information regarding permissions, send a query to the author at catherine@catherinejonespayne.com.

This is a work of fiction. Any names, characters, places, events, or incidents are either the product of the author's imagination or are used fictitiously. Any similarities or resemblance to actual persons, living or dead; events; or places is entirely coincidental.

Visit www.catherinejonespayne.com for more information.

ISBN (paperback) – 978-1-946693-19-8

ISBN (ebook) – 978-1-946693-20-4

Cover Design: Jenny Zemanek, Seedlings Design Studio.
Author Photo: Steven Noreyko.

Visit the author at www.catherinejonespayne.com
Facebook: catherinejonespayneauthor
Instagram: catherinejonespayne

For Eliana. I cannot wait to read the books you write. Remember the most important thing: Always trust in God.

Chapter One

A Monster Tale

"Sea Star!"

My little brother Nathanael swam into the grand dining room and past the coral statues, flapping his fin as fast as he could.

"What?" I asked from where I sat at the elegant dining table across from Father. "Did you and Cyrus play a trick on Quirinia again?"

A month earlier, Nathanael and his best friend had released squid ink in their teacher's classroom. He hadn't stopped talking about it since, even though he'd gotten in *so much* trouble for it—detention at school *and* Father had banned him from participating in this year's duels tournament.

Father frowned at me. I swallowed and shifted uncomfortably in my hammock chair. It hadn't been a *proper* question, and unlike most twelve-year-olds, I—Crown Princess Eliana Hannapola of the great city of Thessalonike, daughter of King Demetrios and Queen Hanna—must always be proper.

But I couldn't help it. I looked back at my brother in anticipation.

Nathanael shook his head, his eyes wide. He stopped to float in front of me and poked my elbow. "Bigger than that!" he exclaimed.

I rubbed my arm and frowned at him. "A bigger trick than the squid ink?"

At two years younger than me, my brother was far more inclined to risk getting in trouble.

Mother cleared her throat.

But Nathanael just shook his head again. "Not a trick, Sea Star. I didn't do anything this time!"

My brother had called me *Sea Star* for years—it had started as a joke, because *Sea Star* sounded so much like *sister*. But I didn't mind that the nickname had stuck around.

I leaned forward, picked a piece of seaweed out of his dark green hair, and flicked it under the table. "Something bigger than a trick?"

"Cyrus saw a monster on the reef!" he practically shrieked, unable to contain it any longer.

"And what exactly was Cyrus doing on the reef?" Mother asked from her seat next to mine, her accented voice stern. "There is no reason for a ten-year-old to be out there by himself."

Mother stared at Nathanael until he squirmed, but then she relented—Mother always relented from being stern. She swallowed a bite of food and added, "He needs to be more careful, or he really might meet a monster out there."

"He did!" Nathanael said, waving his arms. "He said it was big. Not very wide, but really long. Shaped like a shark, sort of. But not a shark. Too long for that and without any fins."

Father furrowed his gray eyebrows. "Shaped like a shark, but not a shark? Did he see a webbed-foot dragon out there?"

"Dragons have fins," I said.

"But they look very different than a shark's fins," Father said. "Perhaps Cyrus didn't recognize them as fins."

Nathanael swam around the table and plunked down into his hammock chair. Because it was just our family eating together tonight, we sat in a cluster at one end of the long table.

The dining room always seemed too big and fancy when Mother and Father didn't have guests. Coral statues lined the edge of the room, and the walls were covered in gold and studded with pearls of various sizes.

Definitely too fancy for everyday use. Not that I was complaining about being a princess. *Most* of the time.

"Not a shark or a dragon," said Nathanael, whacking his fin against the floor. "A different kind of monster. He didn't recognize it. He knows what sharks and dragons look like!"

"What do you think it could be?" I asked, letting my curiosity get the better of me.

My brother just shrugged.

Mother and Father shared a look. I'd seen that look before, and I didn't like it. It meant they thought we were being silly kids.

But Cyrus *did* have a vivid imagination. I wasn't really sure *I* believed him, either. I stabbed my crabcake with a fork and shoved it into my mouth. Chewing gave me something to do while I thought about what Cyrus had said.

No, I decided. I didn't believe him.

Surely he'd just imagined the monster. Or he was telling Nathanael a scary story as a joke.

There might be strange monsters out in the deepest ocean—we didn't really know what lurked out there in the darkest part of the water, past the drop-off—but they didn't come onto the reef.

Here, near the city, we occasionally saw sharks or webbed-foot dragons, and those were dangerous enough.

I shivered at the thought of all those teeth. And dragons had claws too! They didn't swim near the city often, though. I'd never seen a live one.

I did see a dead dragon once. When I was eight, my teacher had the Royal Mer Guard take our class out onto the reef to look at the body of a dragon. The soldiers hadn't killed it—it was already dead when they found it, I guess because it had gotten too old or sick.

The dragon had been huge, probably five times as long as the tallest mer in the whole city. And each of its teeth stretched as big as Father's hand.

Father looked down his nose at Nathanael. "You're not to go out looking for a monster, no matter what Cyrus tells you. Understood?"

"And don't worry. The monster isn't real," Mother reassured us. "I haven't heard of such a thing in my whole life, and I've traveled the ocean."

Nathanael slumped in his seat. "I told Cyrus no one would believe me."

Mother really *had* traveled the ocean. So if she didn't believe that kind of monster existed, I didn't, either.

She'd been raised in a kingdom called Shiloh, far away from our home here in the city-kingdom of Thessalonike. When she was just a little younger than me, she and her family had crossed the ocean to escape an army of invading sirens, and they'd ended up here.

Who'd have guessed she'd meet the crown prince in school and fall in love and end up becoming queen of her new city?

Father reached across the table to squeeze Mother's hand affectionately. I grinned, but Nathanael made a gagging noise.

Then Father turned back to both of us and said, "Don't forget your responsibilities. You know you can't swim wild like other children. You have to grow up more quickly than most. The city depends on you."

"I know, I know," muttered Nathanael, rolling his eyes.

"Especially you, Eliana," Father added.

It was a lecture we'd heard many times. I'd turned twelve a week ago, and I was the oldest child of the king. Someday, I'd rule this city as its queen. And that meant I had to *protect the people*.

Which apparently meant I had to protect *myself* and couldn't take risks like leaving the city often. And since Nathanael was next in line for the throne after me—and would be until I had children of my own—he had to be careful too.

I took my responsibilities seriously—really, I did—but sometimes I thought Mother and Father just used them as an excuse to be strict.

My thoughts drifted to the upcoming duels tournament. I'd been working hard in combat practice. If I could win the whole tournament—first by winning my duels against the other kids my age, then by challenging the older ones competing for this year's Great Pearl . . .

Pictures floated through my mind—Mother and Father saying they hadn't realized how well I could take care of myself. The other kids finally taking me seriously.

The kids at school didn't make fun of me, exactly. Someday I'd be their queen, after all. But they said things, sometimes, that made me feel small.

You get everything you want.

Wish my father was the king—I wouldn't ever turn in my school tablets. The teachers couldn't make me.

You're lucky you don't have to work hard.

The youngest mer in history to win the Great Pearl had been thirteen. If I could win it this year, at age twelve, I'd prove to all of them that I was capable. That I didn't get everything handed to me just because I was a princess.

The duels tournament was just five days away.

Mother reached over and ruffled my long blue hair, and I came back to myself. *Right. We're still talking about Cyrus's monster.*

"But, just to be safe," Mother said slowly, "we'll send a few extra soldiers to patrol the reef tomorrow. In case Cyrus saw a strange-looking shark or dragon."

Father furrowed his brows and tapped his spoon on his plate. "Do you think that's really necessary, my dear?"

Mother gave a firm nod, still talking to Nathanael and me. "Both of you children have that trip out there with your classes in a couple of days. Learning about different kinds of coral, right?"

"Yeah," we said in unison.

"Well, then," replied Mother. "We'll want to make sure it's safe out there before you go."

"Of course," Father agreed, biting into a piece of shrimp.

The lessons on coral didn't thrill me, but excitement tingled in my stomach at the thought of swimming on the reef. It was always so pretty out there. I loved the beautiful colors and all the fish. If we were extra lucky, we might even see a manta ray.

As I thought of Cyrus's monster story, a wave of anger swept through me, and I stabbed another crabcake—a little too hard this time. The more I thought about it, the madder I felt. If mer believed his lie, my class trip to the reef might get canceled. Cyrus could leave the city anytime he wanted, but I couldn't.

At school tomorrow, I'm going to give him a piece of my mind.

I didn't need Mother and Father to have an excuse to keep Nathanael and me even *more* cooped up.

Chapter Two

On the Reef

"Boys," I sighed to my best friend, Lyssa, two days later.

She tossed her magenta hair and rolled her eyes. "I can't believe Cyrus talked about the monster *all day* yesterday. None of us believed him. Why is he always trying to show off?"

"And no matter what we said, he wouldn't let it go!" I groaned. "At least we still get to go to the reef today. I was so afraid they'd make me stay home, but they just sent out an extra patrol to make sure everything looked safe."

"I'm so excited!" she squealed.

Lyssa and I turned onto a busy canal. On either side of us, buildings rose two stories high. The canals were bustling, with mer traveling to school or to their jobs or to the shops. We swam a few tail lengths up from the seafloor—high enough to soar above the dolphin-driven carts heavy with wares to sell in the markets, but still below the line of second-story doors. If we went much higher, Father would scold me for swimming at the top of the city where it wasn't as safe.

Not that anyone had died from a shark or dragon attack since before I was born.

"What are you hoping to see out there today?" Lyssa asked as we reached a quieter section of the canal.

A school of teal fish darted out of a coral garden and rushed past us. I laughed as one of them looped around my head three times before fluttering off.

"I'm excited to see all the fish out there," I said. "There are way more on the reef than here in the city."

"As long as your guards don't scare the fish away," Lyssa said with a chuckle.

I glanced backward and frowned.

Two mermaid bodyguards trailed close behind us. I loved Stasia and Amalthea—they'd lived with us since my first year of school—but sometimes I *almost* wished I was a normal kid who could swim to school alone like everyone else.

"They'll stay far enough away," I said. "They're just keeping an eye on me."

Lyssa shrugged. "You deal with it better than I would. I'd get *sooooo* frustrated if my parents hired someone to follow me all the time. Especially if I could fight as well as you can."

Annoyance boiled in my stomach, but I didn't argue with her. I'd been trained in combat almost since I could swim, and I could take care of myself more than most mer twice my age.

Maybe if I win the Great Pearl in the duels tournament...

But instead of voicing my frustration, I just swam a little faster toward the schoolreef.

We rounded the corner onto the last canal and found our teacher Calandra waiting outside the coral-and-stone building.

Calandra's hair was pink and silver and always seemed to poof out around her head like a crown, or some kind of multicolored anemone. Today, she hovered alongside Quirinia and two other teachers, a sea of students crowding around them.

A few other kids swam past the group into the building, floating jealous glances our way. Their classes were stuck inside the school building, like normal. A trip to the reef was a rare treat, and only the schoolmer aged nine through twelve got to go today.

We reached Calandra's side, and I clutched my netting lunch bag more tightly.

The day was finally here! *Time to see if I can spot a manta ray.*

Lyssa elbowed my ribs. "You remember that coral that looks like branches? I really liked that last time."

"I think I remember where some of it was," I said, scrunching up my face. "Over by the big round coral that's taller than us."

"That's right!" She pressed her palms together in excitement. "I called that one a rock coral, remember? Fishes and wishes, I can't wait to get out there!"

Lyssa and I chattered nonstop, but it still seemed like ages before all the other kids arrived.

"Why is it taking so long?" I groaned, sinking to the sandy seafloor. "Did they get caught in a crosscurrent or something?"

Lyssa rolled her eyes. "Patience, El."

I found an interesting shell and dug into the sand. "You're one to talk about patience."

She stuck her tongue out at me and started braiding her hair.

Finally, Calandra snapped her fingers and called, "Attention! Guppies!"

When Calandra was in a good mood, she called us *guppies*. When she was in a bad mood, she called us *barracudas*.

"Hey, guppies!" she called again. "Eyes on me!" Her poofy hair, which was cut short, bounced as she talked. "I hope you all remembered our trip to the reef today. If not, I trust you've figured it out by now."

The other kids all nodded at her. On the far side of the group, I spotted Nathanael and Cyrus. Hopefully Cyrus would stop talking about the monster. I was *really* tired of hearing the story over and over again.

"Does everyone have a lunch?" asked Jerome, the teacher for the eleven-year-olds.

We held up our netting bags so he could see them.

"Very good." Calandra nodded, and it looked like her hair had taken on a life of its own, as if it were some sort of bouncing animal nodding along with her. "You know the rules. Stay where we can see you at all times. Watch out for any signs of sharks or webbed-foot dragons. Pay attention to rogue currents and any poisonous coral, which you should be able to identify by now. Anyone who wanders off will have detention for a whole month, and I *will* inform your parents. Let's be off, then!"

The group gave a little cheer, and we fell into line behind Calandra and Quirinia, swimming down the canal in the direction of the city gate. The other two teachers took up the rear to catch any stragglers.

"Don't know why we can't swim over the wall," muttered Lyssa.

I shot her a sharp look.

"That keeps us all safer," I said. "It means the guards know who's left the city. If someone gets lost or injured on the reef, we can send out a rescue party. It protects the people."

Out of the corner of my eye, I glimpsed my bodyguards swimming at the back of the group, talking with the other teachers. At least on the reef, they wouldn't be alone.

Soldiers waited at the gate to accompany us schoolmer onto the reef, to help the teachers keep an eye on us and make sure no one wandered off. And, I supposed, to fight off any sharks—especially great sharks, the most fearsome shark of all—or dragons that might be prowling out there.

Or Cyrus's monster. I shook my head, trying to banish the thought to the depths. It was silly. Mother was right. There was no monster.

For one day, I could feel a little more normal. For one day, we'd all have guards watching us.

We're going to the reef!

Lyssa and I kept close to Calandra as we swam down the two-story canals. The classes' excited conversations grew louder as the gate came into view. My heart beat fast.

We're here! I hadn't left the city in nearly a year.

Calandra and the other teachers stopped when we reached the gate and its dozen soldiers—twice as many as usual, so that six soldiers could come with us.

Quirinia said a few words to the soldiers' commander, then moved forward again. Six of the soldiers followed our group out onto the reef.

As the reef opened up in front of me, I gave a little gasp.

All my thoughts about monsters and bodyguards and being cooped up in the city floated away. In front of me were schools of fish, flashing in every color imaginable, and a field of coral in all shapes and sizes.

After a year in the city, I'd forgotten how pretty it all was.

"Fishes and wishes!" whispered Lyssa.

Calandra waved at us, her pink-and-silver hair bobbing atop her head. "You're free to explore for *one* hour to get out your energy. The guards will station themselves in a circle, marking the area you're allowed to swim. *Don't* try to slip past them unless you *really* want detention for a month. I'll call you back when it's time to begin our lesson about coral."

"Come on!" Lyssa cried, grabbing my hand and dragging me forward. "We don't have a moment to waste!"

We flew through the water, moving from fish to fish and coral to coral.

One kind of coral was light brown and shaped like a giant rock. Another looked like bright red fans. And I couldn't even get started counting the hundreds of kinds of fish—huge fish, tiny fish, black fish, pink fish, silver fish. One of the blue fish was *huge*—as big as me, with a big round bump on its head.

I kept my distance from that one.

"There's the coral branches you wanted to see!" I called, pointing.

"Ooh!" cried Lyssa. We swam forward and studied the formation. But it didn't keep her attention for long.

"A turtle!" she squealed, dragging me further on.

Ahead, one of the soldiers turned to face us, marking the spot we weren't allowed to swim past. The turtle glided past the soldier, away from us.

"Not fair." Lyssa pouted, flipping her braid over her shoulder.

Then I heard someone singing—a low, eerie melody that made me feel cold all over. Quillpricks bloomed on my arms. I hadn't ever heard a voice like this before—deep and musical, beautiful but ever so strange.

But before I could ask Lyssa about it, I felt a sharp tug on my hair, and a hand clamped over my eyes. My stomach jolted. We were out on the reef, away from the safety of the city.

And someone was trying to kidnap me.

Chapter Three

A Monster Sighting

All at once, my instincts kicked in. My combat training roared to the surface.

Time slowed, and I felt as calm as a doldrum-still sea. I reached across my body, grabbed the wrist of the mer who was covering my eyes, and twisted *hard*. At the same time, I curled forward, letting my momentum launch the mer over my head.

Without stopping my movement, I slammed the mer into the brown rock coral beneath me.

The attacker—a boy younger than me, I vaguely realized—grunted, then squealed.

"Sea Star!" yelled Nathanael from behind me. "Stop! Please!"

I blinked, staring at the boy who'd pulled my hair. He had a black fin, frightened eyes, and an all-too-familiar face.

Oh. It was only Cyrus, playing a trick on me. Not someone come to kidnap me.

I let him go, but gave him a hefty shove for good measure. "What do you think you're doing?" I yelled.

Cyrus trembled. "I-I'm sorry, Eliana. It—"

Nathanael darted to my side and tugged at the edge of the wrap I was wearing. "It's my fault. I dared him."

I whirled on Nathanael. "You know better than that," I hissed, "and so does he."

My brother bit his lip, looking as nervous as a puffed-up puffer. That giant blue fish with the bump on its head swam past us, indifferent to our fight.

"You don't get to just attack someone like that, even as a joke." I crossed my arms. My heartbeat was starting to return to its normal pace.

"I . . . thought it'd be good practice for the duels tournament," said Nathanael, still tugging at my wrap. "I'm sorry. It was a stupid idea."

I glanced up at the nearest guard, but he looked bored. That made me even angrier.

Scowling, Lyssa shoved her way between my brother and me. "You boys are going to be in *so* much trouble."

Cyrus was floating above the rock coral now, clutching his wrist. His shoulder was scraped, and the faintest trace of blood curled up from the broken skin.

Rage and disappointment crashed through me. *Not blood!*

"Now you've done it," I yelled, pointing at the blood. "We'll have to go back to the city now, because that blood could attract great sharks."

Lyssa huffed at the boys. "I can't believe you ruined our day. We barely had a chance to see anything." She seemed almost as mad as I was.

The guard glanced up at the word *blood*. He studied us carefully, judging the situation.

Nathanael shrank back.

"And what if I'd broken Cyrus's wrist?" I was yelling now, but I didn't care. The boys had scared me—and now we were going to have to cut our much-anticipated reef trip short. My first reef trip in a year!

I hadn't been this angry in a long, long, *long* time.

The guard swam forward, waving us toward Calandra. "Head in," he said lazily. "Go to your teacher. Can't have blood in the water. Against the rules."

A sob choked my throat, but I bit down on my tongue. Wouldn't give the boys the satisfaction of seeing that they'd gotten to me.

"You might *have* broken my wrist," Cyrus muttered, his face and gills paler than normal. "It really hurts."

"Good," I retorted.

It was wrong for me to be glad he was in pain—I knew that. A princess should feel compassion. But right now, I was too mad to think straight.

"Boys," Lyssa muttered.

"Are you going to tell Father?" Nathanael squeaked.

I crossed my arms and stared at him. He shrank even smaller under my gaze, then whirled and tugged Cyrus toward the teachers.

So there.

Nathanael was right about one thing—winning the duels tournament was looking more and more possible every day. Now that my billows of fear had calmed, a burst of excitement surged in my chest, poking out from beneath my anger. Sure, Cyrus was smaller than me, but he'd had the element of surprise. I'd been surprised by someone and still won the fight.

I could practically *feel* the Great Pearl in my hands.

The guard swam past Lyssa and me, mumbling, "Babysitting duty."

My gills flared, and I looked around. There weren't any other guards nearby. That guard *definitely* wasn't supposed to leave us behind like that—*especially* not after Cyrus's scrape put blood in the water. And he shouldn't have just let us fight, either.

I didn't know who the careless guard was, but I didn't like him one plankton.

"Guess we should go in too," said Lyssa. It looked like the news was getting around—the other kids were all swimming in toward Calandra and the teachers. So were the guards.

"Yeah." I turned around to look out one last time at the reef stretching into the distance. All those bright colors. So many interesting things to see.

Then, over the sound of the kids behind me . . .

What's that noise? I tilted my head, listening, and tugged on Lyssa's hand. It was that song again. That unfamiliar voice.

"What?" She whirled toward me.

"Listen!" I hissed.

But the song had gone quiet.

She wrinkled her nose. "I don't hear anything."

I squinted out at the reef. "I thought I heard something. Almost like someone's singing way out there, swimming nearer, then further away," I said, gesturing. "But I guess it was nothing."

Maybe a mer's voice was carrying from the city, or maybe from the kelp gardens further out, where the farmers grew our food. Everyone knew noises could sound kind of strange on the reef. But still . . .

Lyssa looked past me and pointed toward another of those round rock corals. "Oh, look at that crab!" she exclaimed through a yawn. "I've never seen a blue one that big. Sure wish we didn't have to go home yet."

But I was still looking off toward the noise. Or at least where I *thought* the noise had come from. That definitely wasn't where the kelp gardens were.

What *was* out that way? Was that the direction of the drop-off, where the reef ended and plummeted all the way to the bottom of the sea? A shiver like quillpricks darted down my spine.

Then, far away, a shape moved in the water. I blinked, staring at the shape, trying to understand what I was seeing. It was very long, maybe as wide as two mer put together, like a . . . too-long shark without any fins.

Cold fear washed over me.

Cyrus's monster is real.

Chapter Four

INTERRUPTED

"L-Lyssa!" I stammered, tugging at her arm.

"What?" She looked up at me curiously.

"Look!" I pointed just as the monster vanished, swimming deeper into the water, beyond where we could see. But it was still out there. I knew what I'd seen.

It looked more like a webbed-foot dragon than a shark, but it wasn't a dragon. Long. Thin. No fins. Just like Cyrus had said.

Although it did have some sort of spiky fans on its back—maybe those were its fins? They didn't look like fins to me.

"What?" A moment too late, Lyssa stared out over the reef. Her forehead wrinkled. "Sorry, El. Didn't hear anything a moment ago, and don't see anything now. You feeling okay? You must have been really startled by that stupid trick the boys played on you."

"I . . ." What was I supposed to say? That I'd seen Cyrus's monster? Would Lyssa believe me?

Lyssa's face scrunched as she peered harder into the deep blue. I relaxed. She was my best friend. Of course she'd believe me.

At least . . . she'd believe me once she had a chance to get used to the idea.

Another wave of fear crashed over me as I remembered Cyrus's scratch—the blood in the water. The reason we were returning to the city early.

Sharks and webbed-foot dragons would attack if they smelled blood. Could this monster smell blood too?

No time to explain. We needed to get out of here *now*. I'd answer her eight thousand questions when we reached home safely.

"There's something out there," I said. "I'll tell you more later. We have to go. Hurry."

Her eyes grew as wide as a puffer, and she covered a yawn. "Fishes and wishes! What'd you see? A shark?"

But without any fins. The words tingled on the tip of my tongue, but all I said was, "Let's go."

We hurtled toward Calandra as fast as our fins could propel us, past the colorful fish we'd barely gotten to see. When we reached the gathering of students, Calandra shot us a disapproving look but didn't say anything. We were the last ones back.

"Well, then, barracudas," she called in a tired voice. "We'll be off."

For the first time in a while, gratitude flooded me at the sight of Stasia and Amalthea among the soldiers. My bodyguards had been on a different part of the perimeter and hadn't seen Cyrus pull my hair, no doubt, or they'd have stopped him. And then I wouldn't have slammed Cyrus into that coral, and we wouldn't all have to go home now.

Except . . . there really *was* a monster out there, so it was good we were going home. I swallowed hard, looking around at the other kids, the teachers, the guards. Then I tilted my head, blinking. I counted five guards, in addition to Stasia and Amalthea.

Weren't there six before?

"Will you tell me now?" asked Lyssa when we passed the gate and swam into the city.

I felt relieved. We'd made it back to safety without being attacked by the monster. I dismissed the thought about the guards. I must have miscounted earlier.

They usually sent six guards on school trips, but they must have been one short this time for some reason.

I opened my mouth to answer Lyssa, but before I could say anything, a realization hit me as hard as I'd hit Cyrus.

I couldn't *just* tell Lyssa about the monster. I had to tell Mother and Father too. My stomach sank.

If there *was* a monster out there, mer needed to know. Before it hurt someone who ventured past the city walls.

But . . . Mother and Father had been so quick to dismiss Cyrus's story. Even if Lyssa believed me, would they? Or would they dismiss my story too? I rubbed the back of my head. It still stung where Cyrus had tugged on my hair.

And whether or not Mother and Father believed me, they'd almost certainly be stricter after I told them.

They might think I'm lying. They might think I got carried away with my imagination. Or they might realize there really is something dangerous out there.

No matter what, I knew they'd keep a closer watch on me. It felt like something tight was wrapping around my neck, like a fitted wrap that came up too high on my throat.

"Tomorrow," I said. "I . . . have to go home."

Now Lyssa really looked concerned. But I shrugged away from her and swam faster, darting past the other students until I caught up with Calandra. This time of day, the canals weren't as busy. I tapped Calandra's shoulder.

"Yes, Princess Eliana?" she asked.

Her hair bobbed up and down with her words, as usual.

"I'm sorry, Calandra, but I'm not feeling well," I said quickly. It wasn't a lie. I felt sick to my stomach thinking about the monster.

She frowned and rested her fingertips behind my gills to check for a fever. I knew she wouldn't find one, but I waited patiently.

After a moment, she shook her head and said, "I'm sure you'll feel better when we get to the schoolreef. Cutting the trip short was a disappointment for all of us, but we'll schedule another trip right away so we can have that lesson about coral."

We haven't lost our chance to go out on the reef!

At first, I felt relieved, but that didn't last. With a monster lurking out there, the idea of a second trip just made everything worse.

I bit my lip. "I really need to go home, Calandra."

She flicked her fin a little harder, studying me, then shrugged carelessly. "Well, your bodyguards can take you home, no doubt, so I'll say yes. I'll send your schoolwork tablets home with your brother."

"Thanks," I murmured.

I turned and swam back through the crowd of students. I couldn't look at Lyssa or Nathanael or Cyrus as I passed them.

"El!" called Lyssa, but I ignored her.

When I reached Stasia and Amalthea, they glanced at me, looking almost glassy-eyed.

"I don't feel well," I whispered. "Can you take me home?"

Amalthea reached out to check my gills for a fever, just like Calandra had.

"Not sick like that," I told them. "Just . . . home, please."

They glanced at each other, then nodded in unison. I hardly ever asked to go home early. They must have realized this was important.

I let Amalthea loop her arm around me as we swam through the canals toward the palace. She yawned. "Sorry. I got so tired all of a sudden back there."

"Me too," said Stasia. "A wave of exhaustion hit me on the reef."

I almost laughed. I was the opposite of tired. Nervous energy coursed through me, buzzing in my ears. From here, I spotted the pink-and-teal spires.

Almost home. We'd be back soon.

It was still late morning, and the trip home didn't take long without many mer to dodge in the canals. With each turn we made, I felt more and more nervous.

If only I hadn't seen the monster. Then I wouldn't have to tell Father and Mother about it.

We crossed into the palace's coral gardens. My bodyguards started swimming toward the smaller door, the fastest way to the corridor that housed my family's bedchambers.

But Father and Mother wouldn't be there right now. They'd be in the throne room with their advisors. I swallowed the lump in my throat and darted away from Stasia and Amalthea, toward the grand stone doors to the throne room.

"Princess!" Stasia called slowly.

But I ignored her. I swam as fast as I could toward the throne room, so I could blurt the truth to my parents before I lost my courage.

Heart pounding, I glided into the grand room. The ceiling soared high above me, and detailed stone carvings hung on the walls.

I stopped. Mother and Father sat on the two thrones at the front of the room. Six of their advisors perched in smaller chairs on either side of the thrones. Before them floated two mermen, who were arguing with each other.

My parents were judging a case. They were busy. I chewed my lip. I wasn't supposed to interrupt when they were busy like this.

I swam forward anyway.

This is too important.

Mother and Father had told me over and over again that it was my lifelong duty to protect the people, no matter what. And a monster we didn't know anything about was lurking nearby, a threat to the people of the city, to anyone who might venture onto the reef: the kelp farmers and the coral gatherers and the guards who patrolled looking for signs of sharks.

A lot of mer traveled onto the reef every day.

"That was not the agreement!" yelled one of the arguing mermen. "You cheated me out of that money!"

My hands shook as I swam past the mermen. I didn't know who was right or wrong in this dispute, but I did know I had to tell my parents about this monster right away, before someone got hurt.

"Eliana?" asked Mother, interrupting the arguing mermen, her voice gentle and concerned. "Whatever is the matter? Shouldn't you be on the reef?"

Father's face was sterner, his eyebrows ruffled. He looked from me to the two mermen and back at me again. "I trust you have a good reason for interrupting a judgment," he said flatly.

My gills flared with anxiety. Mother and Father stared at me. All the advisors stared at me. The two mermen stared at me.

"I need to talk to you," I squeaked.

"We're in the middle of a judgment," said Mother, tilting her head.

My throat felt hot and tight with frustration. "I can see that."

They gazed at me, waiting for me to continue.

"We had to come in from the reef early," I said, "because . . ." I decided not to muddy the water with the whole story about Nathanael daring Cyrus to grab my hair. "Because someone got scraped and started bleeding."

Mother laughed aloud, her voice lyrical. "Is that what you came here to tell us?"

But Father floated upward, anger in his eyes. "Young lady, this is a place that demands respect and—"

"I'm not finished!" I yelled.

Now I really *would* be in trouble. Making a scene in front of the advisors like this. It wasn't proper. It wasn't *princess-like*. But they weren't *listening* to me!

The amusement fell from Mother's face. "I'm sorry, my dear," she said. "I shouldn't have interrupted you."

I regathered my determination and blurted, "I saw a monster on the reef."

Chapter Five
A Serpent Story

"You saw a shark?" Mother asked in concern.

Father looked more frustrated than ever. And I knew why. My stomach flipped.

If I'd seen a shark or even a webbed-foot dragon—any of the usual dangers—I should have told the guards at the city gate. They knew what to do. They trained all the time to drive off those kinds of threats, to force predators away from the city so they couldn't hurt anyone.

I shouldn't burst into the throne room over a shark.

But this was different.

I shook my head rapidly, willing them to believe me. "It wasn't a shark or a dragon. I promise. It was . . . it was the same monster Cyrus saw. Way longer and thinner than a dragon, with no fins. But it did have these . . . fans on its back."

Mother's mouth fell open a little.

Even Father looked uneasy. He glanced past me, to the mermen who'd been presenting their case.

"Why don't you come back tomorrow morning at low tide?" he said in a tone that brooked no disagreement. "We will finish hearing your case then. And, by the tides, tell no one of what you've just heard. We don't want to cause a panic before we've investigated fully."

They didn't say anything aloud, though one of them grumbled quietly. I glanced behind me and saw the two of them bow, then turn to swim out of the throne room, past Stasia and Amalthea, who awaited me near the entrance. When the mermen neared the door, they both swam faster, each trying to leave first—one ended up crashing into the door.

I didn't want to look at Mother and Father. Not with all the advisors here.

But I had to. I met Mother's gaze first. She appeared sympathetic, at least. Father seemed thoughtful. Hope washed over me.

Would they believe me after all?

"If I may," offered Lady Seraphina, the advisor sitting nearest Mother.

I'd always liked Lady Seraphina. She didn't treat me like a baby the way most of the other advisors did.

"The princess's report," Lady Seraphina continued, "reminds me of a bedtime story my older brother told me to scare me. A long time ago." She chuckled, but then her face grew serious again. "A story of a great monster called a *serpent*. He described it as shaped like a cucumber—long and thin, with giant fans on its back."

I gasped.

Lady Seraphina added, "He said it would wrap up . . . well . . ." She half-smirked. "Wrap up disobedient young mermaids and eat them for lunch. He wanted to frighten me, after all."

The other advisors snorted in laughter, but Mother wrung her hands, her knuckles whitening.

Lady Seraphina studied me carefully. "Perhaps it was just a story, but many such tales contain a plankton of truth, and the similarities between that old tale and the princess's account strike me as peculiar."

I knew I'd always liked Lady Seraphina for a reason.

"Thank you," I mouthed.

She offered me a quiet smile, though her eyes looked troubled. "Why don't we have a battalion of soldiers scour the reef? They can search for signs of anything unusual—to see if they can sight such a creature, or find evidence that fish are being hunted in greater numbers than normal. Anything peculiar they might find."

Another advisor interrupted, "Surely these are the fancies of an imaginative child whose friends have been spinning stories. Why must we work the Royal Mer Guard harder? We don't have enough recruits as it is."

My hands curled into fists.

Lady Seraphina clapped her palms together. "And are you so certain that the princess has been led astray that you conclude we should risk the lives of our citizens by not even investigating?"

"Meant no offense," he said, shrugging.

Mother nodded, glancing from me to Lady Seraphina to Father. "We'll send out the battalion to conduct a search. It's a strange story, but our Eliana is not given to wild tales."

"Indeed." Father stroked his dark beard, as if deep in thought.

I felt warm on the inside. Relieved. They believed me! And the Royal Mer Guard would find the monster. Find the *serpent*, if Lady Seraphina was right.

The word seemed to fit. I'd call this monster a *serpent*, since we didn't have any other name for it.

Father shifted in his throne to look straight at Lady Seraphina. "Tell us of the stories of these *serpents*—any scrap of information that might be true."

Mother held up her hand. "Eliana, why don't you go on home? We'll return to our quarters to be with you as soon as we can. Stasia and Amalthea will take good care of you in the meantime."

Disappointment churned in my stomach.

I wanted to tell Mother that I didn't need anyone to take care of me—especially here in the safety of the palace. And I *really* wanted to hear what Lady Seraphina would say about the serpent stories. But one look at Mother's face told me arguing was pointless.

"No," interjected Father gruffly, "she should go to duels practice early. She doesn't have much time before the tournament—it's what, three days away?"

I gave a small nod. "Yeah, three days."

Father said, "Practice will take her mind off this monster business."

"That's right!" exclaimed Mother. "What a good idea. Eliana, get ready and go to the amphitheater to train with Artemis."

My shoulders slumped, but I nodded respectfully. I swam toward a side door that led toward our living quarters, my mind quickly forming a plan. I *would* go to duels practice early—but first, I wanted to hear what Lady Seraphina had to say.

Stasia and Amalthea met me at the door, but I waved them off.

"I really want to be alone for a little bit," I said quietly. "I need to clear my mind before duels practice so I can fight my best. Could you give me time to rest before you take me to the amphitheater? And . . . could you bring me some fresh sweet puffs? Those would cheer me up."

Stasia folded her arms and Amalthea pursed her lips, training stern glowers on me in unison.

"You should have told us about the monster," Stasia said, suppressing a yawn. "We can't protect you if you keep secrets like that."

Impatience flooded me. If I was going to listen in on Lady Seraphina's stories, I needed to hurry my bodyguards out of here.

"I'm sorry," I said—and I meant it. I should have told them on the reef. "It was . . . overwhelming. I just kept thinking about telling Mother and Father so they could protect the people. I guess I was worried you wouldn't believe me."

Amalthea softened immediately and enfolded me in a hug. "You're always honest, Eliana. Of course we'd have believed you."

A little jelly of guilt squirmed in my stomach. Was I being perfectly honest right now, in my scheme to send them out of the palace?

But I hugged Amalthea tighter and squeaked, "Sweet puffs?" Then I turned to Stasia and added, "And maybe you could pick up my schoolwork tablets from Calandra early, so I can get started on them as soon as I'm back from duels practice?"

With an indulgent smile, Amalthea nodded, rubbing her eyes like she still felt fatigued. Stasia was still scowling, but she whirled and swam down the corridor.

Amalthea squeezed my arm, her touch warm and comforting. "She's angry because she cares about you," she whispered. "She'll be back to normal when she returns with your school tablets. Just . . . tell us about these sorts of things, yes?"

I dug my fingernails into my palms and gazed down at the stone floor. "I'll try. I'm sorry."

Amalthea waved my apology away and darted toward the outer door. "A dozen sweet puffs coming your way," she called. "If I don't fall asleep swimming!"

When she rounded the corner and vanished from view, I paused for a long moment, then flipped around and swam back toward the throne room. My heart pounded. I pushed the door open the tiniest crack, straining to hear.

"—intelligent," Lady Seraphina said. "Smarter than a great shark, certainly. In one of the stories, the serpent didn't eat for weeks at a time. When it got hungry, it started trapping its prey one by one over many days, wrapping the prey in some sort of . . . netting, I think, and stashing it in a cave until it had collected enough for a full feast."

"How would a monster without any hands use netting? Where would it even get netting from?" Mother asked, her tone skeptical.

"Who knows?" said Lady Seraphina. "It's just a story. I'm sure most of the things my brother said about it weren't true. But he was much older than me and had traveled many times to Marbella. Maybe he heard some of the stories there. All I'm saying is that there's a possibility that the creature Eliana describes really exists."

"Perhaps," said Father.

I didn't like the way his voice sounded. Like he wasn't sure he believed me.

He continued, "She's very honest. I'm sure she *thinks* she saw a monster out there. But, more likely, she was fooled by a trick of the light. Since she heard Cyrus's story so recently, she thought it looked like the same sort of creature he described. She's still so young, and children imagine things."

It felt like someone had punched me in the gills.

This was exactly the reaction I'd been afraid of. And it felt even crueler now. Because I'd thought they'd really believed me.

My gills flared. I pulled away from the door, not wanting to hear more. Sadly, I swam down the corridors toward my bedchamber. The stone walls felt cold and imposing, like they might close in around me.

"It's alright," I whispered to myself. "They'll see. The soldiers will find the serpent, and they'll know that I really *saw* it."

I just hoped they'd be able to drive off the monster before someone got hurt.

Chapter Six

IT'S A TRAP

Arriving at the amphitheater, I tightened my grip on my club and popped the last sweet puff into my mouth.

Around the arena, dozens of mer clashed in combat. Everyone was older than me by several years—the kids my age were still at school. Half the fighters sparred with clubs, and the others engaged in hand-to-hand fighting. No one used swords or any bladed weapon—it was strictly forbidden to use a sharp weapon against a living creature, even a fish, inside the city, unless we were repelling an invasion that required us all to fight in order to keep the city from falling.

And there hadn't been an invasion in five hundred years.

Fighting with sharp blades meant more blood in the water—and enough blood in the water would draw great sharks from miles around, bringing a feeding frenzy down into the city canals.

So, we rarely practiced with blades—and only very dull ones, so we wouldn't risk any cuts.

"Princess Eliana!" cried Artemis with an enthusiastic wave. "You're here early!"

My combat teacher broke away from the young merman she was fighting weaponless and swam toward me, dodging a fierce club battle.

Artemis had won the Great Pearl four times—more than anyone else alive. She'd stopped competing for it when she'd left the Royal Mer Guard to start a career as a combat trainer. Her students won the Great Pearl at least half the time. I'd been training with her since I was four.

I offered an unsteady smile. "I . . . left school early because I wasn't feeling well. Mother and Father decided I should come here."

Artemis flipped her dark braid behind her back and tilted her head, lighthearted suspicion twinkling across her sharp features. "You weren't feeling well enough for school, so they wanted you to fight instead of rest?"

When she said it *that* way, it didn't make any sense. But Mother and Father clearly hadn't wanted to start rumors about the monster. Which meant I shouldn't tell Artemis.

I opened my mouth, then closed it.

Stasia darted to my side and rescued me. "The princess had a scare on a class trip to the reef. A boy grabbed her hair and covered her eyes. She made him pay dearly for it. But it still startled her."

"You saw that?" I asked, surprised.

She gave me a wry smile. "I was in the circle of guards, close enough to see you but too far away to intervene before you finished the fight. It was very impressive."

A satisfied smirk crossed Artemis's face. "I hope you didn't hurt the poor child."

"A little," I murmured. "I flipped him onto a rock coral. He got scraped up enough to start bleeding. And I twisted his wrist pretty bad."

Artemis covered her mouth but couldn't hide her proud smile. "Well, serves him right, in my opinion. He should know better than to take on a fierce fighter like you. You used his momentum against him, just like we've practiced."

I basked in her words of praise. Artemis knew I could fight. Knew I was a contender for the Great Pearl. Knew I could take care of myself.

I just had to prove it to Mother and Father and everyone else.

"Let's see your hand-to-hand fighting," said Artemis. "The tournament is in just a few days, and it's your last year to break the record and become the youngest winner in history."

She didn't need to remind me.

I nodded briskly, excitement pulsing through me, and handed off my club to Amalthea.

Father had been right—going to training early had been a great idea. Here, I could lose myself in the acrobatics, the dance of combat, rather than boiling with worry over the monster—the serpent—on the reef.

The serpent wasn't my responsibility anymore. I'd told Mother and Father. They would protect the people.

Surely when a battalion of the Royal Mer Guard went in search, they would find proof that something was out there, just as Lady Seraphina had said.

"Oh!" Artemis put her finger to her lips, as if thinking. "I need to do something first, before we train. How about you swim the perimeter of the amphitheater floor before you stretch? I want you to get a feel for how big of a space it is. Remember, it'll just be you and your opponent here when you fight in the duels tournament. You're not used to that."

"Sure," I said, squinting. Artemis hadn't ever asked me to do anything like that before, but I wasn't about to second-guess the city's best combat trainer. Over the years, a lot of the lessons she'd taught me hadn't seemed important at the time—like the times she'd told me to *pay attention to the eyes*. When I was younger, I thought that didn't make sense. Why waste time looking at my opponent's eyes when I needed to be paying attention to their club slicing through the water?

But as I'd grown in my skills, I'd found I could learn a lot by looking in someone's eyes as I fought. I could figure out which way they were about to swing their club, whether they were tiring, if they were preparing themselves for a tricky move.

And as I looked in Artemis's eyes now, I saw a gleam of amusement.

She was up to mischief.

"Leave Stasia and Amalthea here—I need help with something," my trainer added, waving a hand carelessly.

Stasia arched an elegant eyebrow, but Artemis gestured around the arena.

"It's not like she's going to leave our sight," Artemis pointed out, and both my guards shrugged in agreement. She glanced back at me. "Swim along, now—then come back and stretch."

What is she planning?

I nodded obediently and darted toward the edge of the arena. When I reached it, I glanced back toward Artemis and my guards. They were floating in a circle, deep in conversation. Stasia and Amalthea yawned in unison.

What I wouldn't give to hear what they're saying.

But I decided to swim at a comfortable pace—if I went too fast, I'd tire myself out.

That was another of Artemis's lessons: *Always pace yourself, and you'll make fewer tactical mistakes.*

As I passed a pair of young mermen enthusiastically swinging clubs at each other, I sized up their tactics and shook my head disapprovingly. They were struggling to overpower each other with brute strength, but that wasn't the best way to win battles—there would always be someone stronger out there. A better warrior fought defensively while they assessed their opponent, looking for weaknesses, waiting for the right moment to strike in an unexpected way.

That was how I'd win the duels tournament—I couldn't expect to overpower the adult mer, especially the ones in the Royal Mer Guard. I wasn't stronger than them. I had to outwit them, using my speed and size to my advantage, using their own strength and momentum against them.

I kept swimming.

Every so often, I glanced at Artemis, Stasia, and Amalthea out of the corner of my eye. But they'd gone back to acting like everything was normal.

Finally, I circled the whole arena and swam slowly up to my trainer and guards.

"Are you ready?" Artemis called.

I shot her a triumphant grin. "I was born ready!" I exclaimed.

"We'll just see about that," she said with a sideways smile.

We faced each other for a moment. When she nodded, we each spun in a circle—the formal beginning to a sparring session—and then she lunged at me.

I darted away, and my fin skimmed across hers. She'd almost caught me.

"Nice try!" I said in a teasing voice. "But I'm faster than you!"

She gave a dark chuckle. "No one's faster than me."

"There's always someone faster," I replied, sizing her up, trying to figure out her next move.

This time, she came at me from the right, reaching for my arm. Time slowed as she stretched out, slicing through the water, coming fast—she'd given up some control to attack at top speed.

This is my chance.

My gills flared as I fell back, throwing her attack off-balance at just the right moment. She tried to tilt to the side, to readjust, but I was ready. I grabbed her arm and dove beneath her, swimming the opposite direction. She went into a tailspin, flipping over, and I let go. Her momentum carried her forward, straight into the sandy seafloor.

She grunted, and I darted away to a safe distance, then whirled to look at her. She was hovering above the seafloor, rubbing her wrist.

"Did I hurt you?" I called, suddenly anxious.

"Not a chance, Princess," she said, her voice tight.

I wasn't sure if she was telling the truth or not—was she acting like she was hurt to convince me to let down my guard?

But Artemis could call an end to the fight at any point by surrendering—if she was still fighting, I'd still fight too.

I swam straight at her, attacking on the side of her tweaked wrist. She twisted around and grasped at me with her other hand, then feinted away before I could grab hold of her.

We passed each other without touching, leaving a swirl of bubbles in our wake.

I whirled around again. She was trying to tire me out.

Fight smarter. Another one of her lessons.

Then her lips curled in an amused smile, and I sensed someone looming behind me.

I jolted forward too late. A net dropped over me. I plunged toward the seafloor to escape, but the mass of brown ropes tightened around my body.

I was trapped.

Chapter Seven

DODGE, DART, SPIN

"Stasia!" I yelled, tugging at the net that trapped me. "Let me go! This isn't fair."

But my guard just held the net's mouth closed with a satisfied shrug. "Well, well, well"—she gulped down a yawn—"look what the fishers dragged in."

"I win!" Artemis called, swimming toward us, a grin on her face.

Amalthea, hovering next to us, mouthed, "Sorry."

Seething, I crossed my arms and scowled at them. "No fair. You teamed up on me."

But inside, I was kicking myself. I'd known Artemis was planning some trick. I should have been prepared, but I'd gotten so focused on the fight that I'd forgotten.

Still . . . "We're supposed to be practicing for the duels tournament," I said, my arms still crossed. "And nothing like this is allowed in the tournament. It's always one-on-one."

Artemis's face grew serious. "You can let her go," she said to Stasia.

A mermaid and merman spun past us in a whirl of clubs, kicking up sand off the arena floor and making the water hazy.

Stasia opened the mouth of the net, and I wriggled free. Then I faced Artemis, daring her to explain herself.

At first, she said nothing. I crossed my arms again. "How does this help me win the duels tournament?" I demanded, hot anger washing through me.

"I'm not training you for the duels tournament," Artemis said in a steady voice. "The duels tournament is just a game we host to encourage our fighters to work hard and hone their skills. I'm training you for real life."

Though I didn't budge, something in her words made sense. I chewed my lip and waited for her to continue.

Artemis's angular face softened. "In real life, in a real battle, there aren't rules that say no one can play a trick, or that a group of three mer can't gang up on you with a net. You must remain aware of your surroundings and keep your wits about you. You can't expect a fight to unfold a certain way. That's what I'm training you for, Princess Eliana."

Silence fell between us, and the cries of the fighters sounded even louder in my ears.

"What is your duty as crown princess?" Artemis asked.

A piece of seaweed floated past me, and I flicked at it with my fin, saying nothing.

Her tone grew more insistent. "What do your parents always tell you? What have they drilled into you again and again from the time you were small?"

"To protect the people," I murmured, staring down at the sand.

Artemis swam to me and tilted my chin up. "I'm very proud of you. You've come a long way as a fighter. You have as good a chance as anyone at winning this tournament. But remember this—win, lose, or draw in the tournament, your higher duty endures: protect the people. That is a mission you must never fail at." She paused. "The tournament doesn't matter. Not really. The citizens of Thessalonike—they matter. Each and every one of them. You must always remain on your guard, so that you may always fulfill your duty."

I didn't say anything.

Though I heard the truth in her words, anger still pounded in my chest. My hands curled into fists, and I dug my fingernails into my palms so that I wouldn't snap and say something I'd regret. But as I looked at Artemis's serious expression, my anger began to melt away—a little bit.

"Fine," I muttered. "Can we practice one-on-one now? Even if the duels tournament isn't important compared to my duty as crown princess, I'd still really like to win."

Artemis laughed aloud. "Yes. We can practice for real this time."

I relaxed, and Stasia and Amalthea withdrew to the edge of the arena to watch us, the netting still draped over Stasia's shoulder.

"Did I hurt your arm earlier?" I asked Artemis.

She chuckled and rubbed her wrist. "It stings a little, but nothing I can't fight through. You're stronger than you know, Princess."

The remnants of my anger vanished like squid ink dissipating in the tide. Artemis and I faced each other, assuming our fighting stances. Then she nodded, and we whirled in a circle and dove at each other.

We sparred all afternoon long. Occasionally, my thoughts drifted back to the monster I'd seen on the reef, but for the most part, I blocked that out and obeyed Artemis's command to stay focused on fighting.

In a battle, she said often, *you must block out everything else going on in your life. If you're distracted, you'll lose.*

So I lost myself in the game of battle—dodge, dart, spin.

Artemis won the first sparring session, successfully pinning me to the seafloor, but I won the next two.

We took a short break, and then the school-aged mer arrived. About half the students at school were in combat training—some because they wanted to join the Royal Mer Guard after they graduated, some because their parents wanted them to be able to defend themselves in a fight, some because they wanted a chance to fight for the Great Pearl.

Artemis paired me up with Georgios, a boy two years older than me, for a sparring session. I'd fought him before, and I usually won—he was strong, but not very fast.

We spun and charged at each other. I darted to the side, grabbed his arm at an angle, and pinned it behind him until he cried out that he surrendered.

I grinned and looked over at Artemis, who was watching with an amused grin.

"That was fast," she said wryly. She glanced over the pairs of fighters. "Eliana, you'll fight Beta next. Georgios, you'll take Evander."

Again, my thoughts drifted back to the serpent. Was the Royal Mer Guard searching the reef yet? Would they find it?

But then Beta arrived to spar with me.

"Focus," I whispered.

Beta and I faced each other, taking up the fighting stance, and I pushed away all thoughts of the serpent. The Royal Mer Guard would find it. They *had* to. I'd just focus on winning this fight—and then the whole duels tournament.

I'd win the Great Pearl if it killed me.

Chapter Eight
No Promises

Lyssa grabbed my hand and dragged me to the far end of the schoolreef, near the shallow caves where the smaller kids often played swim-and-seek.

"You *have* to tell me what's going on," she hissed. "You can't keep a secret from me like this. I was *dying* of curiosity last night."

I swallowed hard. Lyssa had known something was wrong yesterday on the reef, when I'd told her I saw something. But I'd left in a hurry to alert my parents to the monster.

"I'm sorry," I said, sinking to the seafloor and digging my hands into the sand. "I panicked. Forgive me?"

She rolled her eyes and threw her head back in frustration. "I'll only forgive you if you tell me! Fishes and wishes, was it a shark? You didn't see a dragon, did you?"

I glanced around. The schoolreef brimmed with kids, from the tiny ones playing with shells to the sixteen- and seventeen-year-olds chattering loudly with their friends. No one was near enough to overhear us.

I spun back to Lyssa and whispered, "It wasn't a shark. Or a dragon."

She stared at me in silent anticipation.

The gills in front of my ears puffed in and out. Why was it so scary to tell Lyssa? Finally, I blurted, "Cyrus's monster is real. I saw it."

"You what?" she shrieked. "A monster?"

I grabbed her arm. "Not so loud! I . . . I think it's called a serpent. My parents are having some guards go look for it. They're going out today."

I'd returned home from combat practice last night, bruised and exhausted, hopeful that my parents would have some news about the serpent. But the Royal Mer Guard hadn't begun the search yet. They'd spend today scouring the reef.

Lyssa opened her mouth, then closed it again.

"Lys," I implored, "please stop freaking out. You're making me nervous."

Her eyes narrowed. "Are you pulling my fin? Is this all some big joke so you can say you fooled me?"

I drew back, feeling hurt.

Even Lyssa doesn't believe me?

"Would I do that?" I asked, my voice small.

"No," she muttered. Then her eyes popped wide again. "Wait, you're saying there's *really* a monster out there? That Cyrus was telling the truth after all?"

I nodded seriously.

"And we were out there on the reef with it?"

I nodded again.

Her hand flew to her mouth, and she glanced in the direction of the city gate—as if she could see through the buildings all the way to the reef. There was a gleam in her eyes I recognized. And all of a sudden, I felt really, really, *really* nervous.

"Lys—" I began.

"What did it look like?" she interrupted.

I paused, remembering the long, thin body swimming in the distance, so far off I could just barely make it out.

"I guess it looked a lot like how Cyrus described it," I said. "And really big. It was hard for me to tell exactly how big, because it was a long way away. But bigger than a webbed-foot dragon, I think. Or . . . longer than a dragon, at least. I think it was slimmer."

"Whoa." She fell quiet, but that look on her face told me she was thinking about doing something that would get us both in trouble.

So. Much. Trouble.

After a long pause, she said, "Maybe we should go find it."

I laughed uproariously.

But Lyssa wasn't laughing.

Abruptly, I grew stern. *What is she thinking?* "You can't be serious," I said.

She tilted her head, then burst into giggles. "Why not?"

I crossed my arms.

She just shrugged at me, still grinning. "El, stop that. You look just like your mother right now."

What's going on? I didn't understand it. Lyssa liked a good adventure as much as anyone, but she wasn't reckless. She sometimes did silly things that got her in trouble, but she didn't love *real* danger. It didn't make sense that she'd want to try to find a monster we didn't know anything about.

"B-because it's not safe," I finally sputtered.

"How do you know?" she retorted.

"I . . ." How could I even answer that question? It was *obvious* it wasn't safe.

Maybe the monster didn't eat mer. Maybe it just ate fish or seaweed. But it was still a giant animal we didn't know anything about. That meant we didn't *know* it was safe, so—for now—we should treat it like a threat to the city.

"Promise me you won't go out there," I pleaded.

She tilted her head and shrugged. "No promises, El."

Panic flooded my chest. "Lyssa, you—"

"Time to come in!" called Quirinia from the door to the school building. The older kids swam inside, still chattering away, and the littlest mer groaned as they left their shells in the sand and sulked into the building.

I stayed where I was and stared at Lyssa. "Promise me you won't go out there—at least not right away."

"Fiiiiiiiine," she replied, flipping her hair. "Not right away, I guess. But you're really being boring about all this."

Boring? I tried to come up with a response, but I didn't know what to say.

Lyssa was just being so . . . un-Lyssa-like.

I didn't understand it, and it worried me.

It reminded me, somehow, of that guard from yesterday. The one who'd left Lyssa and me behind on the wild reef with blood in the water.

Lyssa giggled again, shoved my shoulder, and swam toward the school building. I sat in the sand for a few rapid heartbeats, staring after her.

I didn't know what was going on, but I didn't like it.

Not one little plankton.

Chapter Nine
No Sign

When I arrived home from school, Mother and Father were reclining together in a hammock in our softly lit living room. Mother smiled tenderly at me, the glow from the bioluminary-filled glass lamps reflecting in her eyes.

"How was school today, my dear?" she asked in her accented voice.

I didn't even remember. I hadn't been able to pay attention to my teacher at all. I'd just stared at the tide glass that marked the time, willing the day to be over so I could find out if the soldiers had discovered the serpent.

Nathanael swam in behind me, and I clamped my mouth shut. I hadn't told him about the monster yet. It didn't seem like there was any point in worrying him.

Plus, if I told Nathanael, he'd tell Cyrus, and I'd hear nothing but "I told you so" from both of them for days.

Nathanael glanced from Mother to Father to me. "What is it?" he asked slowly.

I nibbled the end of my fingernail and tried to look innocent.

"Is Sea Star in trouble?" Nathanael asked with a gasp. He was almost smiling! *Traitor.*

"Why do you look so happy about the idea of me being in trouble?" I snapped, narrowing my eyes at him.

"I'm not happy!" His lips turned downward in an exaggerated frown. "It's just that you're never in trouble."

But I swore he was almost gleeful. *Brothers,* I thought in irritation.

"No, your sister is not in trouble," said Mother, giving Nathanael a reproving look.

"Then what's wrong?" he finally asked, shifting uncomfortably.

There was no keeping it from him now. When Nathanael set his mind on figuring something out, he would persist until he succeeded.

I whirled back to my parents and blurted, "Did the guards find anything when they searched the reef?"

Nathanael darted to my side and repeatedly poked my arm. I smacked his hand away.

"Did the guards find *what* when they searched the reef?" he demanded excitedly.

"Eliana—" Father interjected.

"Cyrus's monster," I said before Mother or Father could hush me.

"You mean you believe me?" A grin spread across his face.

I took the plunge. "I . . . saw it on the reef yesterday, right before we had to come back early."

Nathanael floated higher, spinning in a circle. "I told you! Cyrus really *did* see a monster out there! I was right!"

"Enough, children!" called Father sternly. He sat up straight in the hammock. "Eliana, please don't start any rumors. The Royal Mer Guard went looking today. There was no sign of anything out of the ordinary on the reef. The fish don't seem to be alarmed, and there's no evidence of any large creature hunting out there."

"But I *saw* it," I insisted, my heart dropping. "There's something out there!"

Mother pushed herself up from the hammock and swam toward me. "I know you think you saw a monster, my dear. You're not lying to us." She pulled me into a tight hug. "But there's a lot of excitement on the reef, and you'd just heard Cyrus's story about—"

"I saw it," I said again. "I didn't imagine it! I *know* I didn't!"

Mother glanced at Father, and that *look* passed between them again. The look I didn't like. The look that said they thought we were being silly kids.

But this time, the look wasn't about Cyrus and Nathanael.

It was about *me*.

My arms and fin felt heavy, and I blinked over and over again as I looked up at Mother. A lump rose in my throat, as big as my fist and as hard as coral. I couldn't swallow past it.

With a hiccup, I fled the room, darting past Mother and Father down the small corridor that led to my bedchamber. I was about to cry, and I couldn't break down crying in front of them.

I barreled through the privacy curtain that blocked off my room and flung myself into my hammock bed, clutching my pillow to my chest.

"Sea Star!" The privacy curtain swished again, and Nathanael pushed against my hammock.

"Go away!" I yelled. "I want to be alone!"

"Don't cry," he said, swinging my hammock back and forth. "I'm *glad* you saw the monster. They don't have to believe us yet. We know it's really out there. Someday they will, too."

My chin trembled, and I grasped the pillow more tightly. Nathanael poked my arm.

"Don't touch me," I hissed, batting at him with the pillow.

He stopped poking me but didn't swim away. "They'll see," he said. "We'll prove that the monster is out there."

Now you sound like Lyssa.

But I couldn't get any more words out past that lump in my throat.

The lump got bigger when I thought about Lyssa, and I realized it was because I was afraid.

Afraid she'd go out onto the reef looking for the monster and get hurt.

That she'd get hurt because the guards hadn't found the serpent and driven it away from the city.

Unless the serpent isn't still out there. Maybe it went away on its own. Maybe that's why they couldn't find any sign of it.

I liked that idea, even though it meant I wouldn't be able to prove I'd really seen the serpent. Because Lyssa wouldn't be in any danger if she insisted on going looking for it.

I flipped over and looked at Nathanael. "We can't prove it's out there," I murmured.

He gripped the edge of my hammock.

Finally, he said, "Well, someone else will see it soon. And then they'll know it's really out there. They'll know we were telling the truth."

I ran my finger along the rough rope netting of the hammock. "It hurts that they don't believe me," I said softly.

He leaned against the hammock and rocked back and forth. The hammock swayed with him. "Did you notice anything else strange yesterday?" he asked. "Like . . . do you think mer were acting strangely?"

I sat up, suddenly alert and curious. "Acting strangely? Like what?"

"Well . . ." He scratched his head. "My teacher seemed a little strange after we got back from the reef. She just let us talk all afternoon and didn't try to teach us anything. The other kids seemed really tired too."

Biting down hard on my lip, I said, "That guard, the one who was nearby when you dared Cyrus to pull my hair—"

"Technically, I just dared him to put his hands over your eyes," Nathanael interjected.

"Fine," I muttered, shooting him a glare. "The guard who was nearby when you dared Cyrus to *put his hands over my eyes* . . . do you remember the way he acted?"

Nathanael nodded, rocking even harder against my hammock. "You mean the way he *didn't* act? That he didn't tell us to cut it out?"

"There's more," I said slowly. "After you and Cyrus went back to see Quirinia, the guard followed you guys.

He swam toward the teachers and left Lyssa and me behind on the reef by ourselves."

Nathanael's mouth made a small *o*. "But there was blood in the water! And you're not just any student—you're the crown princess!"

I nodded seriously. "Really strange that he left a student out there like that. And this morning at school, Lyssa was talking like she wanted to go see the serpent for herself."

"Serpent?" asked Nathanael. "What's a serpent?"

"Oh! Right. Lady Seraphina called the monster a serpent," I said. "Or, rather, she said the way Cyrus and I described the monster sounded like stories she'd heard of serpents."

"Wait!" Nathanael clapped a hand to his head. "You said Lyssa wanted to go look for the monster herself? On the reef?"

"Odd, right?" I asked.

"I wouldn't expect her to say that," he murmured.

I sat up in the hammock. "It's like everyone's gotten too relaxed all of a sudden," I said. "Except Mother and Father. And I guess everything felt normal at fight practice . . . except Stasia and Amalthea were exhausted after we came back."

"It's just the mer who were out on the reef with us," said Nathanael. "They're the ones who are too relaxed."

He was right. It *was* just the mer who'd been on the reef.

Something about all this didn't make sense yet, but I had a feeling it all fit together like the pieces of a broken coral statue.

"If our teachers and the Royal Mer Guard are too relaxed . . . well, that's a great opportunity for all sorts of tricks," mused Nathanael, but his face was serious—even worried. "But I don't like it."

"Me neither," I murmured. "Me neither."

Chapter Ten

A Mermaid Lullaby

"Eliana?" Mother appeared in the doorway, my privacy curtain swishing behind her.

I sat in my hammock, my tail curled up underneath me, trying to finish the last complex ciphering problem on my school tablet.

The work was taking me longer than normal—my mind kept flitting back to the serpent, and the devastating disappointment that my parents didn't believe me.

"What?" I asked casually, trying to sound like I'd forgotten all about our earlier conversation.

"You should be asleep," Mother chided gently, swimming to my hammock and sitting beside me.

That lump appeared in my throat again. "I'm finishing my schoolwork. I'm almost done."

"I can see that." She gently took the tablet and graphite scrib from me and leaned forward to set them on my little table. Then she put her arm around me. "Your father and I love you very much."

"I know," I said, my voice small. I desperately didn't want to talk about the serpent.

The sense of awkwardness felt like tentacles tightening around my chest.

Mother adjusted my pillow and eased me down, then started singing, "Sleep, little love. The surface fades from gold to black."

It was the lullaby she'd sung at bedtime when Nathanael and I were small—she only ever sang songs here in our family quarters.

"Sleep, little love," she continued in a clear, lilting soprano. "Rest safely, nothing lack."

Nathanael and I didn't sing in public, either. Mother's great-grandmother had been a siren, so Nathanael and I were part siren too.

We didn't have enough siren blood to properly enchant anyone, but our singing voices could draw mer in—beguile them so they thought we were wonderful. If we sang, mer would love us more . . . which was why we didn't sing. It wasn't fair to use our power that way.

"Sleep, little love." She brushed a strand of hair away from my face. "May currents gently rock your bed. Sleep, little love, lay down your weary head. Sleep, little love, tomorrow will be time for jest. Sleep, little love. The fishes bid you rest."

The song ended, and I shifted, leaning my head against her tail. The familiar lullaby felt warm and comforting, a memory of simpler times.

"Tell me a story from when you were my age," I said.

She laughed, a lyrical, lilting sound. "I think you've heard all my interesting stories."

I scooted toward her and laid my head on her lap. "Then tell me about how you and Father fell in love."

Mother's singing had reminded me of that story—a story I'd heard many times before, but one I never got tired of.

"It's past time for you to be asleep," she said, but she smiled with indulgent affection. "But just one story, I suppose." She ran her hands through my hair. "I was fifteen—just three years older than you—and still struggling to get used to life in Thessalonike. The culture here is different in many ways than the culture in Shiloh. Even after I adjusted to the new dialect, it proved difficult to adjust to the way mer interact. Mer speak their thoughts more directly here, rather than talking around problems to be polite."

I looked up and met her gaze. "You've gotten used to that now, I think."

She chuckled as she began braiding my hair. "Yes, I've become quite direct, most of the time. I get things done faster that way. But as a child, in my first few years here, I thought mer didn't like me because they spoke directly to me in ways that would have been unspeakably rude in Shiloh. One day, when I was fifteen, my teacher took me aside after school and lectured me. She said I needed to answer more questions in class. But, at the time, speaking in public—answering questions, especially if I wasn't certain of the answer—wasn't in my nature. I was very shy, and afraid of making a mistake in front of others."

I grinned at the strange idea of Mother being shy.

She continued, "The lecture hurt my feelings, and instead of going home, I fled the city, swimming straight past the guards at the gate without even giving them my name. One of them gave chase, but I lost him by swimming into the kelp forest."

She finished the braid, then began to undo it. "After the guard gave up, I left the kelp forest and swam all the way to the drop-off. I sat on the edge and let my fin dangle down as I looked into the dark, cold water."

Her voice took on a dreamlike quality. "I wanted to swim away—to flee this city I hated so much and live somewhere new. But where could I go? Perhaps, with determination, I could have made it to Marbella, or—with good tides—even to the Seven Kingdoms. But would those places really be better? Or would my sense of awkwardness, the feeling that I didn't belong, just take on a new form? So, instead of swimming with all my strength toward Marbella, I began to sing the lullaby—the lullaby I sang to you and my mother sang to me."

A smile spread across my face. I loved this next part of the story.

"Singing seemed harmless," she said, chuckling ruefully. "I was all alone, far from the city, where no one could hear me. By all my family's rules set up to safeguard our magic, to keep us from abusing its power, I should have been able to sing. But, halfway through the song, I sensed someone behind me."

My heart beat faster.

She continued, "I whirled around and saw none other than the crown prince! He was a year older than me, but we'd never spoken at school—I hardly spoke to the girls my own age, let alone anyone else. And from the look on his face, I knew I'd made a terrible mistake."

"He was already in love with you," I said.

She nodded seriously. "He *thought* he was in love with me. He fell for me in the space of four lines of music, when I had no idea he was even listening. He told me that I had the most beautiful singing voice he'd ever heard."

"But you turned him down."

She absentmindedly braided my hair again. "Of course I did—he'd heard me sing! He wasn't really in love with me. The siren enchantment was at work. I swam away and told him to forget he'd seen me, but he pleaded to at least accompany me back to the city."

"And you said yes to that."

"Yes," she murmured. "That I could agree to."

Despite my sadness, warmth bubbled up in my chest.

She continued, "We swam side by side back to the gate. He asked me what I'd been doing out there by myself. His eyes were so kind, and I answered him honestly—that I felt alone in the city, that I didn't know how to fit in. He said he was sorry I felt that way, and he shared his heart—that he, too, felt lonely. He had friends at school, but it felt like he couldn't get close to his friends the way other mer could, that his rank as crown prince meant it was hard for him to tell what was real—when mer liked him for himself and when they were trying to ingratiate themselves with the future king."

A little pang of sadness for Father resounded in my stomach. I was glad I had a best friend in Lyssa—we'd been best friends since we were too small to care about status, and we were going to be best friends forever.

Mother said, "When we reached the city gates, I told him I was sorry, and to forget about me. Then I fled into the canals."

"But he didn't forget about you," I replied.

A soft smile played on her lips. "No, he didn't. The next day, he saw me. I was floating by myself on the far edge of the schoolreef, and he was surrounded by chattering mer. But we locked eyes, and I saw his deep loneliness. After school, he found me. He asked if I'd permit him to say something."

I grinned.

"When I said yes, he told me how drawn he felt to me. You can't imagine the guilt that flooded my stomach. He asked if we might spend some time together, to see if I might, in time, come to feel the same way about him. When his eyes met mine, it was like a whole school of fish were flitting around in my stomach. A handsome, kind prince, pursuing me! But, deep down, I knew he wasn't really in love with *me*. So, even though I was supposed to keep our siren magic a secret, lest mer hate us for our power or suspect us of spying for a siren army, I blurted the truth: that my great-grandmother was a siren, and that the prince only felt drawn to me because he'd heard me sing, and that I couldn't let him fall in love with me, because it would be a lie. Then I stared at the seafloor and waited for him to leave."

"But he didn't leave," I said.

"No," she replied, joy etched on her face. "When I finally looked up, he was still floating there. He looked so thoughtful. Finally, he asked how long the effect of my siren magic would last. Surprised by the question, I replied that the enchantment—if one could really call it an enchantment—should begin to wear off at any moment, but that some residual effects could last for about three months, if the stories passed down in my family were true. And then he asked a question that set my heart beating faster than I thought possible: Could we be friends, then, for a year?"

"And then you asked what would happen at the end of a year!" I exclaimed.

Mother loosened my braid yet again and stroked my head.

"I did," she said. "And he replied that we would swim over that drop-off when we reached it, but that we could remain merely friends, if that's what we wanted when the time came. And so we became friends. Good friends. For him, it meant the whole ocean that I'd had the opportunity to use my voice to sneakily ingratiate myself with him but hadn't taken it. We saw each other's loneliness—me, in my shy isolation, and he, who felt isolated even when he was surrounded by admiring mer. And at the end of the year, he told me his admiration had only deepened, that he was drawn to *me*, not just my song, as if by a strong current, that he'd fallen in love with me—but that I need only say the word and he'd never speak of it again."

"But you'd fallen in love with him, too," I said with a contented yawn.

"Yes," she said. "Your father is handsome and kind and smart and funny and dutiful. I was halfway in love with him from that first day on the reef. But by the end of a year, I knew I loved him desperately."

"And you've been in love ever since!"

She bopped my nose. "That's right," she said, looking deeply into my eyes. "I love your father, and your brother, and you more than anything. Nothing will ever change that. I see so much of your father in you, Eliana. You're brilliantly smart and deeply dutiful, too."

I knew she was trying to reassure me because of how upset I'd been that they didn't believe me. It almost worked.

Almost.

She kissed my forehead.

"Sleep, little love," she whispered. "Dream of happy tides."

She moved from my hammock, dropped a dark cloth over the glass bioluminary lamp, and swished out of my room.

I lay there, trying to hold on to the happy feelings, but Mother's visit hadn't washed away my dread.

Even though I'd worked hard at fight training and tired myself out, I tossed and turned in my hammock, worrying and worrying. I was worried about the serpent. Worried about Lyssa. Worried about the whole city.

What if the serpent is still out there? What if it eats someone?

Chapter Eleven

A Monster Lullaby

After a while, I drifted into a half-sleep.

But I kept jolting awake, lurching out of vague dreams that the serpent was coiling its long body around me and wrapping me up in netting, like in Lady Seraphina's stories.

I also dreamed of that song I'd heard on the reef. The low, unfamiliar voice. There was something cold and terrifying, but somehow familiar, about it... but I couldn't put my fin on exactly *what*.

When I woke up, I blinked, looking around at my bedchamber. Everything was just as it should be.

My room didn't have a window, but a thin line of bioluminaries near the ceiling gave off enough light to see the contours of the room. The fancy mirror standing near the wall. The coral wardrobe that housed all my wraps—though a few wraps lay discarded on the floor in front of the wardrobe. The three netted hammock chairs in a circle around a small table. The big stone chest that housed all the toys I didn't play with anymore but wasn't ready to give up.

Everything was normal. So, why did it feel so strange?

The song, I realized. Even though I was awake, I could still hear the song.

It wasn't a dream.

I scooted out of my hammock and darted to the table, pulling away the seaweed cloth that covered my lamp—a glass sphere coated inside and out with bioluminaries. In the gentle glow of the light, everything felt brighter and safer.

But I can still hear the song.

The melody was quiet. I could just barely make it out. But it was there, unmistakable. The same faint music I'd heard on the reef.

I held up the lamp and looked at the tide glass. *Early morning.* Stasia or Amalthea would come in soon to wake me for school.

If I moved quickly, maybe I could sneak out to the window in the front hallway. I wouldn't leave the palace, but maybe I could see . . . something. Figure out where the song was coming from.

I poked my head into the corridor and looked left, then right.

No one stirred at this hour. I swished past my privacy curtain, slowly turning left, disturbing the water as little as possible with the flicks of my fin. I passed Stasia's room, then Amalthea's, then Nathanael's, then the two rooms that housed Nathanael's bodyguards.

Abruptly, the song stopped.

I stilled, listening. Maybe it had just grown fainter.

But no, I decided. The strange voice wasn't singing anymore. Still, *maybe* I could see something. I swam forward again, faster.

After another turn, I spotted a familiar door at the end of the corridor. This door opened into the front hallway. There was sure to be a guard on the other side, protecting my family while we slept.

I paused, tilting my head. How would the guard react to seeing me this early in the morning?

I didn't *think* they'd stop me as long as I didn't try to leave the palace. I swam forward again.

Almost there.

The door opened from the other side. I stopped, my heart pounding. A mermaid, her long hair tied back in a braid, swam through the door and quietly closed it behind her.

This hall was very dim. The bioluminaries here really needed to be replaced—the light-up plankton had aged and begun to die off.

But the mermaid almost looked like . . .

"Mother?" I squeaked.

My mother stopped and drew herself up to her full length. "Eliana? What are you doing here? Why aren't you asleep?"

I opened my mouth but didn't say anything.

She swept forward and pulled me into a hug, her touch warm and comforting. "You heard that song, too, didn't you?"

I stiffened but let her hold me. "Yeah, I think it woke me up."

I could feel her tension—the worry rolled off her in waves. She was afraid. And that scared me more than anything else.

"Well, I don't want you to worry about it," she said firmly. She let go and looked at me. "Your father and I will get it all figured out. You just go back to sleep."

"I want to help." The words burst out of my mouth before I could stop them. I wasn't sure what I could do, but . . . "You and Father have told me probably a million times that my job is to protect the people. Something is happening, and—"

Mother squeezed my shoulder. "Your *father's* job, and mine, is to protect the people. Someday, that will be your job. The most important task of our lives is to prepare you to take on that responsibility. But you shouldn't worry about these things yet."

"That's not what Father says," I insisted. "I'm the crown princess. I already have responsibilities."

She toyed with the end of her braid, looking almost sad. "And your first responsibility is to keep yourself safe. Your second responsibility is to learn all you can so that, someday, when your father is gone, the people will have a good and wise leader. And then you will train up your own eldest child to take your place."

My mind lingered on the song, but I snorted. "You make it sound like Father isn't a good and wise leader."

A smile danced on her lips. "You know what I mean, Eliana. Your father is a great king. And you will be a great queen. I have no doubt of that."

I wanted to ask her why she thought I'd be a great queen, since she believed that the serpent didn't really exist, that I'd let my imagination swim wild on the reef.

But the lines around her eyes were already taut with worry. I didn't want to add to her concerns.

So I just said, "I really do want to help, if I can."

With a little chuckle, she bent over and kissed me on the forehead. "I'll let you know if there's anything for you to do. Deal?"

Even though I was sure she wouldn't actually give me anything to do, my heart felt a little lighter.

"Thanks," I said.

She pushed me, sending me floating down the corridor. "It's almost morning. Go get ready for school. Stasia will be terribly worried if you're not in your chamber when she comes to wake you."

We swam toward my bedchamber, and I gave Mother one more hug before I swished back through the privacy curtain.

Trying to put the strange song out of my head, I flitted to my wardrobe and threw open the doors, selecting the wrap I wanted to wear to school that day—teal, with just a little bit of sparkle to it.

I changed, then grabbed my comb and raked it through my long blue hair. Floating over to the mirror, I inspected my reflection and nodded.

Perfectly proper, as a princess should be.

With time to spare—I'd gotten up early, after all—I swam to my table, grabbed my completed school tablets, and placed them in my netting bag.

Then I reached for the two thin stone tablets that remained unfinished and sank into my hammock chair. I didn't have to turn these tablets in for another few days, but I figured I might as well get started on them.

The first was for ciphering, one of my favorite subjects. I moved quickly from one ciphering problem to the next. My graphite scrib scratched across the tablet, leaving a black marking on the stone. I always found it a satisfying sound.

I lost myself in the work and finished the last problem on the tablet, exclaiming, "So there!"

When I glanced up at the tide glass to check the time, my hand flew to my mouth.

I'm late!

Then I frowned, my brow furrowing in confusion.

Where were Stasia and Amalthea? *They should have come in to wake me already.*

I floated up from the table and darted through the privacy curtain.

The hall was quiet. I looked left and right again. No one bustled around the living quarters.

What's wrong?

I bit my lip and swam left until I reached Stasia's doorway. Tilting my head, I listened. I could just make out the sound of gentle snores.

I wrinkled my nose and swam to Amalthea's room. She wasn't snoring. I knocked on the doorframe.

"Come in," called Amalthea in a lazy voice.

Now I was *really* alarmed. This wasn't normal. None of this was normal. Stasia and Amalthea always made sure I got to school on time.

The privacy curtain fluttered as I swam into Amalthea's room. She lay in her hammock, a soft smile on her face.

"Princess," she said warmly.

I looked at her tide glass. It told the time accurately. She had to know how late it was!

"What are you doing?" I asked slowly.

"Getting started on the morning," she murmured in that lazy voice.

"But I'm late for school!"

Her gaze flicked up to the tide glass, and she chuckled. "Oh, I suppose you are. That's funny."

"That's *funny*?" I demanded, aghast.

I didn't see anything funny about the situation. I was about to be late to school, for the first time all year!

I backed out of the room and burst through Stasia's curtain. "Wake up!" I called. "I'm late for school."

Stasia grumbled and flipped over to face me. Her eyes met mine, and she squinted, struggling to focus. "Time to go?" she asked, blinking slowly.

My gills flared in and out. "We're late," I said again, more insistently.

She nodded, blinking harder. "Be . . . ready soon."

I raced out of her room and paused, floating in the empty corridor. *Nathanael.*

With nausea washing over me, I hurried into my brother's room to see if he, too, was behaving strangely.

Nathanael was curled in a small ball in his hammock, which, by itself, wasn't unusual. His deep-sleeping was legendary, and his guards always struggled to wake him in the mornings.

But it *was* unusual that his guards weren't rousting him from sleep by now.

"Wake up!" I called, shaking his shoulder.

He started, then jolted upward. "What? What is it? Sea Star?"

"We're late!" I said for what felt like the thousandth time that morning.

He looked up at the tide glass, closed his eyes and shook his head, then looked at the tide glass again.

His mouth dropped open. "Why didn't Silas wake me?" he demanded, rubbing the sleep from his eyes.

My hands trembled. I looked from my brother to the tide glass.

"Something's wrong," I said. "Stasia and Amalthea didn't wake me, either."

His eyes popped open wide. "Is everyone dead?" he whispered, horrified.

"What?" I drew back. "No. They're...fine...I guess? Stasia was still sleeping, and Amalthea was acting...lazy. Like she didn't realize it was important to get going."

The privacy curtain rippled, and Stasia appeared in Nathanael's doorway. Her hair was wild, floating in every direction, and she still wore her rumpled sleeping wrap.

"There you are dear," she said, smiling. "Should we get going soon?"

"Aren't you going to change?" I asked.

She glanced down at her wrap, then shrugged. "This seems fine to me."

Nathanael and I stared at each other, our mouths falling open in shock. Always-proper Stasia, leaving the palace in her sleeping wrap?

Something was terribly, terribly wrong.

Chapter Twelve

Late for School

We *should have been* late for school, but we weren't.

Because the whole *city* was late.

My brother and I swam to school together through the strangely half-empty canals, leaving Stasia far behind when she wouldn't hurry to keep up.

Nathanael's guards and Amalthea had been too tired to come at all.

As we swerved around a corner, careening onto the canal that would take us to school, Nathanael whispered, "Quirinia's going to give me extra school tablets for sure. She hates it when kids are late."

"Calandra doesn't usually give extra work as punishment," I said, fighting the sinking feeling in the pit of my stomach and trying to swim faster. "But she's going to tell me she's disappointed in me."

"Ouch," Nathanael replied with a sarcastic half-grin. "Is that supposed to be worse than doing extra schoolwork? Because it feels like extra schoolwork is worse."

"Hey." I elbowed him. "Just wait until you're in Calandra's class in a couple years. Her *disappointed* look is legendary for a reason. It makes you feel like you're sinking off the edge of the drop-off."

But when we arrived, there was no extra schoolwork from Quirinia and no legendary look of disappointment from Calandra. In fact, I didn't even *see* Quirinia or Calandra.

School should have already started, but the teachers still hadn't called the students inside. Kids floated in groups on the schoolreef, chattering in languid voices.

Nathanael poked my arm six times in a row. "Uh . . . Sea Star?"

"I know," I said grimly, watching the surprising scene. I tilted my head to listen in on the conversations.

The kids closest to us were talking about the song from last night. Most of them had slept through it, but word was getting around.

"Sounds like it was beautiful," drawled an older girl named Jocasta, huddled with her friends at the edge of the schoolreef. "Wish I'd heard it."

Her friends nodded in lazy agreement.

Nathanael and I eyed each other, then drifted together from group to group, listening in. *Everyone* was talking about the song, but no one seemed worried about what it meant.

As the schoolreef filled up with students, I looked around for Lyssa, but she was even later than we were. In fact, a *lot* of kids seemed to be late.

And so did the teachers.

I searched for Lyssa again. Then for the teachers.

Two teachers were here already, one who taught some of the littlest schoolmer and another who taught sixteen-year-olds, though neither of them seemed in any hurry to get school started.

And still no sign of Quirinia or Calandra.

"None of this makes sense," I whispered to Nathanael, gazing around the schoolreef. "It's like . . . they don't care about anything. Everyone's acting like . . . like that careless guard from the reef trip."

He tugged at the edge of my wrap, and I didn't even stop him. "I'm liking this less and less, Sea Star," he said nervously.

"Me too," I murmured. "Let's think." I sank down onto the sandy seafloor. "What could be going on?"

He dug a scooping shell into the sand. "I haven't heard of anything like this happening before."

"Me neither." An uncomfortable feeling twisted in my stomach. "But there've been a lot of odd things happening recently."

"The monster." He held up one finger. "The way everyone's acting funny." He held up a second finger.

I reached out and ticked up his third finger. "The song."

"What song?" He put the third finger down.

"The song that all the kids are talking about?" I asked, raising an eyebrow.

"Oh, I guess I wasn't paying attention to what they were saying," he said. "I was watching how they were acting. Everyone seems so lazy."

I bit my lip. "You didn't hear music on the reef two days ago?"

He shook his head emphatically. "Cyrus and I were pretty busy."

"Last night? Did it wake you up?"

Again, he shook his head. "You know I'm a deep sleeper."

A clique of older kids swam past us.

A sharp-featured mermaid in their midst yawned and said, "My sister—the one in the Royal Mer Guard—was on night-patrol duty, so she heard it. She thought it was so interesting that she came home early to tell me about it. She woke me up! Isn't that funny?"

Nathanael and I jolted, staring at each other as the kids swam on.

"A night-patrol soldier leaving her post?" Nathanael whispered.

"That could get a soldier kicked out of the Royal Mer Guard," I said, feeling suddenly cold.

"No!" He crossed his arms, and his voice got louder. "Not *could*. That *would* get a soldier kicked out of the Royal Mer Guard. She left her post, and now her sister's talking about it like it's the most normal thing in the world? What's going on? Why is everyone acting so strangely?" He slammed his shell down onto the seafloor.

A peculiar thought unfurled in my head like an anemone. "I wonder if . . ." I said slowly. "If . . . maybe the better question is why aren't *we* acting strangely, too?"

My brother picked up his shell and began to dig again.

After a long pause, he said, "I hadn't thought about that." He looked around the schoolreef. Stasia had finally arrived. So had Calandra. But no sign of the other teachers or of Lyssa.

I chewed my pinky fingernail, worry nibbling at me. Why wasn't Lyssa here yet? She hadn't left the city to go looking for the monster, had she? She'd *promised* me she wouldn't go yet.

"Yeah," Nathanael said after a moment, "why are we the only two mer in the city who can see that everyone's acting funny?" Then he whirled to face me. "What if *we're* the ones acting funny and we don't realize it?"

I shook my head fiercely and gestured at the other kids and the teachers. "No. Look at them. This is *not* normal."

"Why are we the only ones who can see it, then?" he asked helplessly.

Mother's face flashed in my mind, and relief filled me.

"Mother and Father can see it," I said after a moment. "I found Mother in the halls early this morning, during the mysterious song, trying to figure out what was going on. She heard the song and was worried about it, just like me. She said they'd take care of it."

"So, maybe it's some kind of royalty thing?" he asked, squinting at me.

I considered his question. "Maybe . . . but that doesn't make any sense, does it?" I clasped my hands, trying to think through the situation. "We royals have a special job and a lot of responsibility, but we're not *really* any different than anyone else."

"Well, none of this makes any sense, Sea Star." He threw out his hands.

He had a point.

A tiny silver fish darted past Nathanael into my hair. I batted at it, and it lumbered away, jerking a little from side to side like it couldn't see straight.

"El!" Lyssa called, swimming toward me with slow strokes of her fin.

Lyssa!

"Hey!" I turned my attention to my best friend, relieved she was here and not out on the reef searching for the monster. "What took you so long?"

She stared at me, then shrugged. "Just took me a while to get ready this morning, I guess."

"Did you hear the song last night?" I asked, stuffing down my frustration at her careless attitude.

Another long stare from Lyssa. "What song?"

Guess that means she slept through it. That's good, right?

I clenched and unclenched my hands. "Remember the song I thought I heard on the reef?"

She squinted, then understanding washed over her face. "Right! Yeah, I remember you talking about that."

"I heard it again last night," I said. "Lots of people did."

"Oh, how lovely," she said. "Wish I heard it. I love music."

I fought against the frustration bubbling in my stomach.

It wasn't Lyssa's fault that she was acting this way. Something was happening to the city. Lyssa was just caught up in this strange current. But I wanted to shake some sense into her.

"Oh!" said Lyssa, brightening. "You said you heard the song on the reef?"

Dread curled in my chest, but I answered, "Yes."

"Maybe the monster is singing!" She curled a strand of hair around her finger.

It was the first sensible thing she'd said since we left the reef. Except . . . animals couldn't sing, could they?

"Let's go look for it!" she exclaimed triumphantly.

I groaned. *Not that again.* "Don't go without me!" I blurted.

I didn't think I'd convince her *not* to go, but maybe I could delay her until we figured this out.

Backing away from Lyssa, I nudged Nathanael. "But I can't go with you to the reef today. Nathanael and I have to go home early," I said.

"Oh?" Lyssa looked disappointed. "Why?"

Nathanael glanced at me, confusion written on his face. He opened his mouth to protest, but I shoved his arm to warn him to stay quiet.

"Something important to do at home," I said to Lyssa. "We'll see you tomorrow, then we'll go out to the reef together! Sound good?"

She shrugged and nodded. "Yeah, let's plan on that."

I tugged Nathanael away.

When we were out of earshot, he whispered, "What are you talking about, Sea Star? We don't have to go home. And you can't go out to the reef tomorrow!"

"I was just making an excuse," I said as we reached the edge of the schoolreef and looked down the empty canal. "Our teachers haven't even started class yet. They probably won't realize we're gone—and if they realize it, they won't care. We need to talk to Mother and Father about what's going on."

"Do you think there'll be combat practice tonight?" he asked.

The duels tournament was . . . tomorrow! *How can it be so soon?*

But it suddenly didn't seem *quite* so important. "Probably not," I said. "There isn't even school today. Not really."

Nathanael seemed to consider this as we swam off the schoolreef, right past Stasia. She was staring at a piece of floating seaweed and didn't even notice us. Quillpricks tingled through me.

"Do you think Lyssa's right about the song?" he asked.

"That the serpent is singing?"

"Yeah."

"Um . . ."

We swam down the canal, between the quiet buildings that rose up on either side.

This time of day, everything should be busy, packed with mer going this way and that. But it seemed like half the city remained asleep. The stillness unsettled me.

Finally, I said, "I don't know if the serpent is singing or not. But I do think that the song and the serpent have to be related somehow. After all, I saw the serpent *right* after I heard the song. What are the odds that two unheard-of things happening at the same time wouldn't be related?"

"What are the odds everyone in the city would lose their minds at the same time?" he grumbled.

We turned down another canal, and the palace's spires rose in the distance, practically sparkling in the light that stretched down from the rippling surface.

I swam a little faster. "Let's hurry."

Chapter Thirteen

BEWITCHED BY SIRENS

When Nathanael and I arrived at the door to the throne room, we pulled to a sudden stop in unison.

"Do you think they'll be mad that we came home early?" he whispered.

I stared at the giant door, a ball of netting tangling in my stomach. I *really* didn't want to get scolded again. The first time had hurt my feelings enough.

"Um . . . I don't *think* so," I said, wincing. "We can explain that school isn't actually happening."

Still, better to peek in first, I decided.

I floated forward and poked my head around the edge of the door.

Father sat slumped in his throne, his hair out of place and his crown missing. His wrap was rumpled and too casual—the sort of thing he'd wear while spending private time with our family, not while conducting official royal business.

My heart stuttered and sank. *Oh no. Not Father, too.*

Only about half the advisors were present at all, and two Royal Mer Guard generals hovered near the thrones.

But that wasn't what caught my attention the most.

Mother was floating directly in front of Father. *Yelling* at him.

I pulled back and stared in shock at my brother.

"What is it?" he squeaked.

"Mother and Father are fighting," I hissed.

His eyes popped open wide. "In the *throne room*?"

I nodded, horrified.

His jaw dropped. "With the *advisors* in there?"

"Yeah," I said, swallowing.

Of course Mother and Father *fought*. All married couples fought, as they'd told us many times.

But I'd only ever seen my parents fight in private, in our own family quarters. If they found a disagreement in public, they excused themselves to discuss the matter behind closed doors.

The king and queen must present a unified front to the people, after all.

So they never let anyone see their petty squabbles, except Nathanael and me and the trusted guards who lived in our quarters with us.

And even then, they rarely yelled.

But now Mother and Father were fighting in the throne room itself, in front of advisors and generals.

Or, rather, Mother was fighting with Father—Father was half-flopped over in his throne. The world was turning completely topsy-turvy.

I put a finger to my lips and crept back toward the door.

"Demetrios, can you hear yourself?" Mother shouted. "The generals saw a merman leave the city by swimming over the wall while that wretched music played early this morning, and they somehow did not think to inform us of this or to send out a search party until now? Our own daughter heard and saw something on that reef. Every person in this city is acting like they've been bewitched by sirens! And you insist that nothing is wrong?"

A merman left the city by swimming over the wall? Uh-oh. A whirlpool opened up in my stomach.

Father mumbled his reply.

The generals, to their credit, looked uncomfortable. But not nearly uncomfortable enough, in my opinion. Only Mother seemed to grasp the seriousness of the situation.

Every person in this city is acting like they've been bewitched by sirens.

Mother would know. She was one of the only people in the city who'd fled a siren attack.

Nathanael poked my arm. "We should go," he whispered.

Though I wanted to listen a little longer, I'd heard enough.

With a sad half-smile toward Nathanael, I drifted away from the door. We swam silently into the coral garden and sat on the seafloor amid a cluster of coral that branched up like fans.

"Did you hear all that?" I asked, gazing up at the shimmering light dancing on the surface far above us.

"Yeah . . . and no one seemed to care but Mother," Nathanael said with a shudder. "Not really."

I picked at a hangnail on my middle finger. "So, it's just Mother and you and me that see how crazy everything's become. Not all four of us."

"So, not a royalty thing."

"No," I murmured. "Not a royalty thing."

"Can we fix it?" he asked, his voice small.

Determination flooded me. "We *have* to fix it. And we will. I just don't know how yet." I pressed both my hands against my head. "Thinking."

If Mother knew what we were up to, she'd tell us we were just kids, that it wasn't our responsibility to save the city yet.

But I couldn't sit down and do nothing. Not anymore. I'd seen Father in there. He wasn't acting like a king. He was being influenced by whatever was making everyone lazy and careless.

Was it magic? Poison? What was changing everyone's personality?

Mother would do what she could to help, of course, but I was the *crown princess*. Someday I'd be queen of Thessalonike. Father had told me over and over again that my first and most important job was to protect the people.

Since something was keeping Father from protecting the people right now, I had to fulfill that duty for him.

I was a princess. First in line to the throne. I was *born* to do this. I just needed to think . . .

My head snapped up. "Do you remember what Mother said in there? About how everyone is acting?"

Nathanael squinted at me. "When she was talking to Father?"

Nodding, I asked, "Can you remember her exact words?"

He wrinkled his nose. "Something about sirens?"

"Sirens," I hissed, snapping my fingers. "She said it's like everyone's been bewitched by sirens."

"Ohhhhhhh." My brother's eyes widened. "Like when she was my age."

"Yeah, just like that." I felt sick to my stomach. "Mother and her family fled Shiloh right before the sirens overthrew it."

He continued, "Most of the mer didn't leave, because they were enchanted by the siren song. They couldn't understand that anything was wrong, no matter how many times Grandfather tried to tell them. So Grandfather took Mother and Uncle Simeon, and they swam away as fast as they could."

I struggled to remember the details. Mother had told us, but it wasn't a story she spoke of often. I think it hurt her to remember.

"Some of the other mer left, too, didn't they?" I asked.

"Yeah," said Nathanael. "A few. Most were bewitched by the sirens, though. Mother and Uncle Simeon and Grandfather weren't bewitched only because—"

"They were part siren," I finished.

"And we are too," he exclaimed, understanding gleaming in his eyes. "Which is why we don't sing in front of anyone—we only sing in private, in our family quarters."

"So, that strange song must mean there's a siren out there," I whispered, aghast. "The city is falling under siren magic. And we're not affected by it because of our siren blood." I looked back at the palace. "We need to find out more about sirens."

"Maybe we should ask Mother?"

I quirked my lips. "Do you think she'll tell us right now, with everything going on?"

His shoulders slumped. "No. She'll know we're up to something."

I hit my fists against each other. "Is there anyone else who can see what's going on? Or anyone who could tell us more about sirens?"

"I wish Grandfather were still alive," he murmured. We'd lost our grandfather almost four years earlier.

"And I wish Uncle Simeon wasn't the ambassador to Marbella," I added. "There's no way we could swim all the way to Marbella to ask him about sirens."

We fell into a long silence.

Then a bubble of inspiration hit me. I pushed myself off the seafloor, suddenly confident. "I know what to do next! Let's go!"

Chapter Fourteen
THE STORY CARVER

The old story carver sat slumped over his table, resting his head on his arms. "Lord Dryas," I called hesitantly from the doorway.

His gills twitched, and his gray tail curled more tightly around the base of his hammock chair.

"Lord Dryas," I said again, swimming into the room.

Whether he was siren-enchanted or not, surely he had information that could help us. We needed to solve this mystery—and soon.

Preferably before the duels tournament.

I sensed Nathanael creeping into the room behind me.

Reaching the story carver's side, I practically yelled, "Lord Dryas!"

The elderly merman snorted and sat up. "I'm awake."

I studied his face. He looked too tired and relaxed. But his eyes appeared *almost* clear. And more mer had been traveling in the canals when we swam here.

Which made sense! I knew from Mother's stories that the effects of siren magic wore off with time. Which meant we needed to ask him questions *now*, before the song started up again.

"We need to hear a story," I said.

Lord Dryas gazed at me in confusion, then glanced up at the tide glass.

"Shouldn't you youngsters be in school?" he asked. He rubbed his eyes. "I think I've been dreaming."

"We really need your help," I said. "It's important. Official royal business."

Well, *semi*-official royal business, anyway.

Surprise flickered over his face, but I just stared at him. I *hoped* my expression looked fierce. That he'd take me seriously and help us.

He leaned back in his hammock chair. "Well, it's not every day that royalty needs my help. What do you youngsters need to know?"

I silently rejoiced. If there were any good tides from this citywide laziness, it was that the adults weren't asking us too many questions.

"You've been the most famous story carver in the city for a long time," I began.

His eyes twinkled. "Since before you were born, Princess Eliana."

I hovered at eye level with him. "So, you've probably learned a lot of stories about sirens, haven't you?"

A shadow crossed his face. "Too many, I'm afraid. And some of them too frightening for youngsters."

Though I bristled, I tried to keep my tone as steady and soothing as possible. "I'm the crown princess," I said. "It's important that I know everything about sirens."

A wrinkle appeared in the middle of his forehead. "Why would you need to know about sirens, Princess?"

"Don't worry about that—just tell me what you've heard about them."

He squinted at me, but then yawned. "Of course, Your Highness."

The siren bewitchment had won out. Lord Dryas stared blankly at the half-finished stone tablet in front of him.

Before we'd arrived, he must have fallen asleep while carving.

"Tell me what sirens can do," I said.

"Well," he began, relaxing back into his hammock chair, "sirens are just another kind of mer, you know."

I nodded. Of course I knew that.

"Some people think that sirens only have mermaids in their ranks—no mermen—but that's not true. I assume that rumor started because of the way they sing—their mermaids and mermen alike sing with higher voices than most other mer."

I wrinkled my nose. The mysterious song hadn't been in a particularly high key—if anything, the notes had been low.

Did that mean this wasn't siren magic?

Why is the city falling under an enchantment, then?

And what about the monster? Surely there couldn't be both a siren *and* a serpent nearby at the same time.

Too much of a coincidence.

Lord Dryas continued, "Sirens are exceptionally beautiful, with delicate features and fins that glint with strands of gold and silver."

I nodded again, sneaking a glance at my own blue fin. Shades of light and dark blue mixed together in swirls, but no gold or silver.

"Tell me more about the sirens' voices," I said, hoping we'd learn something that could help us put the pieces together.

A dreamy expression overtook his face. "Have you ever floated at the surface, Princess?"

"No," I said with a laugh. "Mother and Father would lock me in the palace if I tried something like that."

He smiled softly. "Someday, if you go to the surface at night, you'll see a great black expanse far above, at the top of the whole world, dotted with pinpricks of light. Stars. The sirens sing with the voices of the stars themselves."

I blinked a few times. That didn't mean anything to me. Although it did make me want to see these *stars*.

He picked up his carving and began to whittle it.

"Sirens also have fast reflexes—they react quickly to things," he said. "They're powerful warriors in battle. Most sirens are perfectly peaceable, of course, but their reputation is overshadowed by the siren clans devoted to war. They go from place to place and raid, attacking cities as they search for wealth or sources of magic. Sometimes they attack a smaller, weaker city or settlement just to hone their skills of warfare."

As they search for sources of magic. I'd have to think more about that. "Do they . . . ever have monsters with them?" I asked.

He thought for a moment, then shook his head. "Not in any stories I've heard."

No real answers, then. Disappointment flooded me.

"What about serpents?" I asked. "Do you know any stories about them?"

He paused for a long time.

I let my gaze wander to the carvings around the room, each one showing a different scene from a story.

There were dozens of carvings here, on small tablets and large ones. Some of the carvings were even bigger—etched on huge sheets of rock that stretched to the tall ceiling.

Lord Dryas carved and sold scenes from stories. He'd even done the massive carvings that hung on the walls of the throne room.

Some of the stories were simple, but most told of great moments in the history of the city.

As a queen, would I ever do anything worthy of being carved in stone?

I hoped so.

Lord Dryas cleared his throat. "Serpents. Now that's a monster I've not heard about in a long time."

Hope filled me. "What do you know about them?"

"Are they long and narrow, without any fins?" Nathanael asked.

"But with some sort of fans instead?" I added.

"Quite right, Your Highnesses." Lord Dryas reached for a blank tablet and a thin carving knife. "I'll draw one for you."

With quick flicks of his wrist, he carved a shape into the tablet.

The creature in the picture seemed to take on a life of its own as he whittled with deft strokes. As its form became clear, I stared at it.

There it was. No mistaking it. This was the monster I'd glimpsed on the reef.

A serpent.

Chapter Fifteen
How to Fight a Monster

I gripped my wooden club as Nathanael and I swam into the amphitheater for fight practice.

I'd been worried the arena would be empty when we arrived, that the city's newfound laziness would mean no one would bother to show up.

But about half as many fighters as normal whirled around the arena, and I was relieved to see Artemis giving pointers to a pair of girls along the edge.

"Are you sure we should be here, Sea Star?" Nathanael asked, tugging at the edge of my wrap. "Does the duels tournament even matter anymore? And with the city acting so weirdly, will they even bother to hold the duels tournament?"

I tightened my grasp on my club. "Well, of course the duels tournament still matters," I quipped. "And hopefully we can fix everything *before* the tournament. But that's not why I wanted to come here."

Nathanael floated in front of me and tilted his head in silent question. "Sea Star?"

A handful of students entered the arena, swimming past us.

I looked back at my brother. "I want to learn how to fight a monster."

His eyes widened. "By yourself?" he squeaked.

Raising my chin, I said, "If I have to."

For a long moment, we stared at each other. Then he shook his head and reached toward me. "No, Sea Star. You won't have to fight it alone. If it comes to that, I'll fight with you."

We clasped each other's forearms, making a solemn Thessaloniken promise. "Let's hope it doesn't come to that," I said. "Let's hope Father comes to his senses and the Royal Mer Guard drives it away."

"What about the singing voice?" Nathanael asked. "What are you going to do about that?"

Artemis finally glanced over, then started swimming toward us. I waved at her.

"Well," I answered, "we'll figure out who's singing and why. And then we'll make a plan to take care of it."

Artemis reached us and gave a brisk nod. "Glad you're here," she said, yawning. "I've been so tired today, but I think I'm finally starting to wake up. Let me find you sparring partners."

"Wait!" I exclaimed.

"Hmm?" She looked at me curiously.

My mind raced for an explanation that would make sense. "I . . . think you were right, yesterday," I blurted. "When you talked about how the tournament doesn't really matter."

"Oh?" she asked, looking amused.

The words tumbled out of my mouth, and, deep down, I knew they were all true. "The people of this city matter. My duty to them matters. That's what all this training is about."

She and I locked eyes, and I continued, "I'd like to win the duels tournament and prove myself to Mother and Father, but I don't want to focus all my training on hand-to-hand fighting against one single opponent. That's not what real battle is like. But . . . we haven't been invaded in generations. A king or queen hasn't had to lead the Royal Mer Guard into battle against an army for hundreds of years."

She raised an eyebrow. "Where is this going?"

"I know there are invading armies out there in the ocean and that I need to prepare myself to face them," I said. "But I was thinking about the threats the city really *does* face on a regular basis."

This time, she chuckled. "And what threats are those?"

"Monsters," Nathanael and I said in unison.

When Artemis looked skeptical, I added, "You know—sharks and webbed-foot dragons, mostly. Plus, the ocean is so deep—who knows what else is out there? I know how to fight other mer. What do I do if I ever have to fight a shark or a dragon?"

Artemis's eyes lit up.

At first, she didn't say anything. Then she nodded slowly, pride filling her eyes. "You're really starting to understand what's important, Princess Eliana. And you make a good point. As soon as the duels tournament is over, we'll focus on the tactics the Royal Mer Guard uses to fight sharks and drag—"

"Can we start today?" I asked.

Her eyebrows knitted together. "The tournament is tomorrow. Don't you want to be sharp for that? Learning new tactics like this is a risk. It might throw you off. We can start as soon as the tournament is over."

"I'm sure," I insisted, begging her with my eyes. *Please take me seriously.* "I'm as prepared as I'm going to be for the duels tournament. I want to be prepared to do my duty."

"I want to learn too!" Nathanael piped up. "I'm not allowed to compete this year, anyway, because I pulled a prank on my teacher."

Artemis seemed to consider this, then yawned again. "Very well. Let me grab three dull blades. I'll be right back."

She swam away, and Nathanael whirled toward me.

"Blades?" he whispered.

"We've sparred with dull blades before," I said, though I felt surprised too.

"Sure. We had to learn about fighting with blades in case there's some sort of huge invasion. But if she's having us practice with dull blades to fight a monster, that means . . ."

I finished the grim thought. "That if we're fighting a monster in real life, we might have to use sharp blades."

Artemis reappeared, a net draped over her shoulder, and handed us each a short sword in a sheath, an extra club, and a weapons belt. "Tie the belt around your waist," she said. "You can hang the blade and your clubs on it."

I pulled the sword out of its sheath and examined it. The blade was a little longer than my forearm, carved of rock, with an edge so dull I didn't think it could slice an octopus tentacle.

I re-sheathed the sword, then tied the belt so that it hung just below my waist, at the very top of my tail scales. My heart pounded faster as I slid the sword and both clubs into the belt.

"When you're fighting a monster," said Artemis. "The first thing to know is that you'll want some backup weapons. If you're fighting an army, there are lots of weapons everywhere. If yours breaks, or you get disarmed, you can scramble to find another one. But if you're fighting a webbed-foot dragon, if something happens to your weapon, you have to find whatever you can and use it to fight. That means you're fighting with tools you're not used to—tools you haven't trained with."

"Improvising," I offered.

"Exactly. That puts you at a disadvantage. And if you're fighting a webbed-foot dragon all by yourself, you're already at a disadvantage."

Nathanael raised his hand. "What if we're fighting a webbed-foot dragon alongside other mer?"

Artemis quirked her lips. "That's not very likely to happen, although I'll teach you those tactics too. But we don't send our royalty out to the reef to turn away a webbed-foot dragon. If you're fighting a shark or a dragon, something has gone terribly wrong."

"Like what?" Nathanael asked.

She shrugged. "Maybe the Royal Mer Guard is busy defending the city from another attack, or you stumbled on an angry shark while swimming on the reef, or—tides forbid—a dragon somehow managed to slip past the Royal Mer Guard into the city and you're the first fighter to take on the monster."

Nathanael and I nodded seriously.

Or if no one believes that there's a monster on the reef.

"Most of the time," Artemis continued, "if there's a problem with a monster, we'll send out a contingent of the Royal Mer Guard to take care of it. Neither of you will have to fight it directly. So today, let's focus on what you do if you're fighting a monster by yourself."

"Or maybe with one other mer," I said.

It made me a little nervous to second-guess Artemis, but we needed to learn the right tactics. "Mother and Father don't let us go onto the reef by ourselves. Right now, they barely let us go on the reef at all. But even when we're older, we'd always have someone with us out there. So, how would we fight it with one other person with us?"

"Sure. That makes sense." Artemis yawned again, covering her mouth. "I'm sorry," she managed. "I'm really tired today. I hope I'm not getting sick."

Neither Nathanael nor I said anything.

"So," said Artemis, "if you're fighting a monster, it's a good idea to have at least one blade—don't stab the monster unless you absolutely have to, especially if you're close to the city, because its blood might attract more monsters—and two clubs and a big net."

Chapter Sixteen

Lyssa Lulled

"Princess," said Amalthea, rustling my privacy curtain. "Lyssa's here to see you."

"Be right there!" I called, setting down the school tablet I'd been halfheartedly working on since getting home. I hadn't been paying much attention to my schoolwork—I'd mostly been thinking of the problem of the monster and the song.

But Lyssa didn't wait for me to come to her. No sooner had I pushed away from my little table than the curtain swished and Lyssa flounced in.

"El!" she cried, throwing her arms out wide.

Relief twinged in my chest, and I hugged her tight. The Lyssa in front of me seemed just like the Lyssa I remembered.

Was the song's enchantment finally wearing off? Everyone had gotten a little more normal as the day stretched on. I'd even overheard Amalthea and Stasia quietly discussing how tired they'd been that morning.

They hadn't *quite* seemed to understand how odd they'd acted. But it was a start. Maybe everyone was finally coming to their senses again, and we could focus on driving away the serpent from the reef. The song didn't have to wear off all the way. Just *enough*.

"Did you hear the news?" she asked, darting onto my hammock bed and curling her tail beneath her.

"What?" I shifted my chair to face her.

"Someone disappeared!" she exclaimed.

"I did hear something about that," I murmured, leaning forward and wringing my hands, feeling suddenly anxious again.

"Mer were talking about it in the canals when I swam home." She wrinkled her nose. "At first I was worried it might be you—where *were* you all day? Were you preparing for the tournament tomorrow? Funny thing, I didn't even notice you weren't there until after lunch. But I swear I saw you this morning. I just can't quite remember..."

"Well, that hurts my feelings." I stuck my tongue out at her. It didn't *really* hurt my feelings, because none of this was Lyssa's fault. On a normal day, Lyssa and I did everything together. Her forgetfulness was just one more sign that the city was in trouble.

"Anyway, I was thinking more about that monster from the reef," she said.

I buried my face in my hands. "Not this again," I groaned.

She *still* wanted to go out onto the reef? Even after the song's enchantment had partially worn off?

She sat up and crossed her arms. "Not what again?"

Well, if she's not *thinking about going to the reef, I certainly won't put the idea into her head.* So I just shrugged. "Sorry. It's been a long day. What were you thinking about?"

"I don't know." She held up her hand and studied her fingernails. "Was just thinking about the monster. It's..."

I waited patiently, but she didn't finish her sentence. "It's what?" I finally asked.

She looked up at me again, and her expression was almost... worried.

"It's just that I feel funny today," she said. "It's like my thoughts have been cloudy. My mind's been like... you know how hazy the water gets when a whole bunch of sand is kicked up?"

I nodded. "Of course."

"My thoughts are hazy like that. I didn't notice it earlier, but now I'm thinking more clearly."

This was progress!

I didn't know what to say, so I just smiled patiently at her. Things were going to be normal again soon.

Lyssa clapped her hands. "Oh, and Calandra noticed you were absent after lunch."

So I'd get in trouble for skipping school, after all. I winced. But it couldn't be helped now. And once we put a stop to whatever was going on, I'd never skip school again.

That had to count for something.

Right?

The curtain rustled, and Stasia appeared in the door, her face serious. "Princess, you need to stay inside for the evening. Someone spotted a webbed-foot dragon on the reef, very near the city. Lyssa, when it's time for you to go home, I'll escort you. We don't want any children in the canals alone."

I stared at Stasia. *A webbed-foot dragon?*

Not what I'd expected. Unease coiled in my chest. I *had* seen a serpent, right? Was there a dragon now, too? Two monsters? Or had a mer mistaken the serpent for a dragon?

Or—I felt hot in my throat and stomach at the thought—had *I* been mistaken? What if I'd seen a webbed-foot dragon and mistaken it for Cyrus's monster?

I didn't *think* I'd made a mistake.

But I just said, "Of course. I'll stay here. Is the Royal Mer Guard going to take care of the dragon? Drive it away from the city?"

"Your father called out a contingent of soldiers. They're assembling at the armory as we speak. The city should be safe by tomorrow at the latest," she replied, nodding crisply.

"Thanks!" I exclaimed.

She disappeared from the doorway, no doubt gliding down the corridor to alert Nathanael and his guards to the danger on the reef.

Lyssa's forehead crinkled again. "I'm trying to think," she murmured. "Fishes and wishes, something's not right."

I closed my eyes, summoning a picture of the monster I'd seen. It *couldn't* have been a dragon. *But—*

"There isn't a dragon out there," Lyssa said firmly.

I tilted my head, curious. "What makes you say that, Lys?"

"If the monster you saw was a dragon, you'd know," she said, rubbing her temples. "You wouldn't confuse it with a monster you hadn't even heard of before."

"But someone who glimpsed the serpent might think it's a webbed-foot dragon," I whispered, "because that's the monster they'd expect to see."

"Yeah!" Lyssa nodded, her eyes brightening.

She added, "Like that time when I was little and I swam up to another mermaid with violet hair because I thought she was my mother. But I wouldn't see my mother and think that she was just some other mermaid with violet hair."

"Which means there probably isn't a webbed-foot dragon," I said slowly. Part of me felt relieved, and another part felt afraid. "A mer saw the serpent, and it didn't make sense to them, so they thought they saw a dragon."

Lyssa fell quiet again, twisting a strand of hair around her finger. Then she said, "I still think we should go find it."

I shook my head fiercely. "Lys, the Royal Mer Guard are going out to find it right now. They're trained soldiers. And Mother and Father would never let me out of the palace again if I went looking for it."

Plus, there was something out there I didn't understand. This had to do with sirens, somehow—even though it didn't all make sense yet.

What if a clan of warrior sirens lurked on the reef, waiting for us to investigate?

A group of soldiers stood a much better chance than Nathanael, Lyssa, and me alone.

Just a few days earlier, all I'd wanted was to win the duels tournament. To prove myself.

Now everything felt upside down. *I hope this will all be over soon.*

"Isn't it your job to protect the people?" Lyssa asked. "Isn't that what your father is always telling you?"

My head snapped toward her. Her eyes were as clear as I'd seen them today. She'd broken through the murky water in her mind and was seeing that things weren't alright.

"The Royal Mer Guard is taking care of it," I said insistently.

"Something's wrong, El," she whispered. "You know it's true."

All at once, I heard a melody that was becoming too familiar. Distant notes of music in a low, haunting key.

The song.

I looked helplessly at Lyssa. Her expression clouded, then relaxed. She leaned back in my hammock and listened to the music with a soft smile on her face. My curtain rustled again, and Nathanael appeared at my side. His gills pulsed, and he hugged himself tightly.

"You hear it this time," I whispered.

He nodded solemnly. "And Silas told me about the dragon. But . . . I don't think there's any dragon."

"I don't think so, either," I said.

With a gesture at Lyssa, he said, "Silas fell asleep almost as soon as the song started too."

I glanced at Lyssa, startled, and saw she'd drifted off to sleep.

Nathanael swam over and poked my arm. "Do . . . do you think there are sirens on the reef?"

"Why would you think that?" asked a soft voice from behind us.

I froze.

Mother.

Chapter Seventeen

SIREN SONG

Mother swam through the curtain, her posture cautious, her expression filled with fear.

She looked first at Nathanael and me, then Lyssa, who still slept in my hammock.

With a serious face, Mother drifted across the room and sank into the other chair at the table, near me. She reached out and touched my cheek with the back of her hand.

"What did you overhear?" she asked. "Yesterday when you brought news of the monster to the throne room?"

"Two days ago," I replied in a small voice, trying to avoid her question.

She blinked a couple times, then managed a chuckle. "So it was. These past days have been a blur, haven't they?"

She paused, waiting for my answer.

"Yeah," I murmured. "Really a blur."

Her lips tightened into a thin line. "What did you overhear?" she asked, gently but insistently.

I looked down at the table and shifted uncomfortably. "You told Father and the advisors that everyone was acting like they'd been enchanted by sirens," I murmured.

"Mmm." She chewed her lip.

"And that makes sense, since we're part siren, and the three of us aren't affected by the song."

Her shoulders sank a little, and her voice grew distant and troubled. "Like Shiloh. My father and brother and I left before the attack."

"You don't have to talk about it," I said in a small voice.

"My mother had already died, of course." She shifted in the chair, and her voice cracked. "But my friends . . . I begged them to come with us, and they refused."

My heart went out to her. I couldn't imagine leaving Lyssa behind like that. It would shatter me.

"So, is the song being sung by a siren?" I asked, cold fear gripping my heart. "Are we about to be attacked?"

"It's not a siren," she replied, her forehead creasing. "That's the strangest part. It doesn't sound anything like a siren. The voice is far too deep." She shook her head. "But Thessalonike is an isolated city. Only Marbella also sits in this part of the ocean, and it takes days to travel from there to here. We three are the only mer in the city who are part siren, as far as I know. And we're the only three I've seen who are unaffected by that terrible song. That's not a coincidence."

Nathanael and I locked eyes.

Mother continued, "It may not be a siren's voice, but it's still a siren song, somehow. Still that same magic."

"So, it's up to the three of us to stop it?" Nathanael asked. "Since we're the only ones who aren't affected by it?"

Mother leaned across the table and tucked a piece of floating hair behind his ear. "The enchantment wears off with time. Your father understood the danger right before the song started back up and lulled him into laziness again. After the enchantment wears off this time, we'll have a chance to explain to him and the generals, and they'll act."

A horrible, foreboding fear wafted over me. "But what if the song . . ."

She studied me, her gaze piercing and intelligent, like she could read my thoughts. "What is it?" she asked softly.

"What if it's sung while the soldiers are searching the reef?" I blurted. "What if the monster gets them? Or what if there *are* warring sirens out there, with different voices than the ones who attacked Shiloh? What if they attack our city?"

"I don't think there are sirens out there." She rested her chin in her hands. "I think the monster you saw—the serpent—is singing."

I blinked, astonished. *The monster is singing?* Lyssa had suggested that, too. But it surprised me to hear it from Mother. "Why do you think that?" I finally asked.

"Sirens rarely travel alone," she said, staring at my bioluminary lamp. "They're attached to their clans. And they certainly don't *sing* alone—singing together multiplies their magic and makes the bewitchment stronger. But the song enchanting the city? There's just one voice—and like I said, it doesn't sound like a siren."

"If a siren's not singing, why is everyone acting this way?" Nathanael folded his hands so tightly his knuckles turned white. "How could someone else have that magic?"

Mother looked at each of us in turn. She was thinking about something. Probably she was deciding how much to tell us.

"I'm the crown princess." I crossed my arms, hoping I looked more grown-up. "I'm going to need to know these things eventually. And if you tell us, we can help you think through the problem. Maybe Father and the Royal Mer Guard can take care of it later, after the enchantment wears off, but no one else can help you come up with ideas *right now*."

Her nostrils flared, but the stress lines around her eyes relaxed. "You're both getting older." She hesitated, then said, "The city I grew up in was home to more kinds of people than just mer—all sorts of different people. Do you know what caecelias are?"

"No," Nathanael and I said in unison.

"They're a lot like us mer," she said, "but instead of a bottom half that looks like a fish's tail, they have the tentacles of an octopus."

Despite the seriousness of the situation, Nathanael giggled. Even I smiled at the mental picture.

A person with octopus tentacles? That sounded so funny. But maybe that was just because I wasn't used to it. Maybe my fish fin would look silly to a caecelia.

"Well," Mother continued, "a group of caecelias in the city—in Shiloh, where I grew up—conducted a famous show. They were magicians who had discovered how to enchant an animal to talk." Mother smiled at the memory. "They had fish and a dolphin. Even a small shark."

"Oh," I whispered. It was starting to make sense. Something Lord Dryas, the story carver, had said about warring sirens echoed in my head: *They go from place to place and raid, attacking cities as they search for wealth or sources of magic.*

Mother said, "Of course, a fish cannot speak with its own voice. It has no voice. But each animal in the show sounded very much like one of these caecelia magicians. They'd enchanted the animals to speak with the caecelias' voices—though the quality of the voice was different for each fish. Most of the fish had high-pitched, even squeaky, voices. The shark spoke in gruff, low tones. The dolphin had a singsong lilt."

"And the sirens attacked Shiloh to steal that magic," I said suddenly.

Her lips tightened. "Have you been talking to Lord Dryas?"

"We asked him about sirens," I admitted. "He told us the warrior clans sometimes attacked while looking for magic to steal."

"I don't know for sure why they attacked Shiloh," murmured Mother. "We left and didn't look back. But if they stole the caecelias' magic, who knows how many animals they've enchanted to sing like sirens?"

"Maybe they enchanted the serpent." The idea coiled through my mind like octopus tentacles. "But that might mean the sirens are here, after all," I gasped. "Are they using a monster to attack us? Are we about to be invaded?"

"I'm sure they're not," she said. "If there were an army of sirens nearby, we'd hear more voices—the voices of the sirens themselves. In the days leading up to the attack on

Shiloh, there were hundreds of voices. And they didn't ever stop."

Rubbing my forehead, I said, "So . . . it got away, or they let it go? And it made its way here?"

"It's a strong possibility," said Mother.

I ran my hand through my hair. "We just have to convince the Royal Mer Guard to drive away the monster before it hurts anyone."

She didn't say anything, and I remembered that a merman had already disappeared. A sick feeling twisted in my stomach. Had the serpent lured him with siren song? Was that how it hunted?

What had Lady Seraphina, the advisor, said about serpents? I was too upset to remember it clearly.

We have to convince Father and the Royal Mer Guard to drive away the monster, or kill it, before it hurts anyone else.

Chapter Eighteen

TOGETHER

I DECIDED TO SLEEP on the floor beneath the hammock rather than wake Lyssa and send her home.

After all, her parents would be too siren-enchanted to miss her, and it didn't seem safe to take a sleepy, lazy Lyssa out in the canals at night.

What if the serpent came into the city to hunt?

Besides, if she stayed in my room overnight, I'd know she hadn't gone out to the reef by herself.

I drifted in and out of sleep, but didn't hear the serpent's song again. That was something—a note of hope.

Maybe in the morning, Father will be clearheaded enough to send the Guard after the serpent, and they'll take care of it before it starts singing again.

But the next day, Stasia and Amalthea didn't wake me.

I woke late, but not terribly late. With a long look at the tide glass, I dressed for school, even though I hadn't decided whether I was going. I looked again at Lyssa, still sleeping contentedly.

I should make sure *she* got to school, at least, and let her parents know she'd spent the night with me. At some point, the enchantment would partially wear off and they'd worry.

My thoughts churned like a storm as I swam to Nathanael's room.

He was curled up in his hammock, hugging his pillow to his chest. He looked so peaceful.

I didn't want to pull him out of his good dreams and into the real world.

But it's time to get up.

I tugged the pillow away, and his face scrunched into a scowl. He curled into a tighter ball in the hammock.

"Wake up!" I hissed.

"Don't wanna," he mumbled.

"I need to talk to you," I said, poking his arm like he always poked mine.

He batted at the air as if trying to find the pillow I'd snatched.

I leaned toward his ear and hissed, "It's about the serpent."

At that, his eyes popped open.

"Alright," he muttered, stretching out to his full length, then flopping onto his stomach and rubbing his eyes. "Serpent. That's important, isn't it? We've got to do something about the serpent." He yawned cavernously.

I tossed him his pillow and backed away, hovering halfway between the floor and ceiling. "You want to go to school today?"

He stuck his tongue out. "Do I ever want to go to school?"

Fair point. "Well, I think you can skip it today," I said. "What's the point of school if Quirinia won't teach you anything because she's enchanted by the siren song?"

He yawned again. "I like the way you're thinking. Does that mean I can go back to bed?"

I darted forward and stole his pillow again. "Not so fast. We've got a job to do."

His shoulders slumped, and he reached helplessly for the pillow. "I thought you'd say something like that," he muttered mournfully.

"Can you stay with Mother while I take Lyssa to school? I don't trust anyone else to get her there safely right now."

He stretched to his full length, then sat up. "Yeah. Wait, why do you want me to stay with Mother?" he asked in confusion.

"Even though we might be the only ones who can help, she's trying to shield us from what's going on. She's not going to tell us everything, so I want you to be here when she talks to Father—which she'll do as soon as the enchantment starts wearing off."

Nathanael squinted at me. "She's just going to tell me to go to my room," he protested.

I crossed my arms. "Tell her you want to help her convince Father that something serious is happening. If that doesn't work . . . I don't know—listen from the corridor if you have to."

He hiccupped, staring at me in shock. "*You*, of all mer, want me to listen in on someone else's conversation?"

Shifting uncomfortably, I said, "I know it's not a great thing to do. But a merman was so enchanted by the song that he swam onto the reef, probably going straight to the monster. The future of the city—mer's lives—might depend on what we do today. I'll be back as soon as I can."

Take Lyssa to school. Pay a quick visit to her parents. Hurry back to the palace.

As soon as the song wore off, we'd help Mother persuade Father of the danger. Then Father would send the Royal Mer Guard out to fight the serpent, driving it so far away that its song couldn't reach the city, or killing it if necessary.

Everyone would wake up from the bewitchment.
We'd all be safe.

Nathanael and I wouldn't have to break all the rules by going out to the reef to face the serpent ourselves.

Nathanael stretched out again. "Yeah, I guess I can do that."

We sat in silence for a moment. Then I handed him back his pillow and said, "I'm glad you're my brother."

He took the pillow and managed a half-smile. "I'm glad you're my Sea Star. We'll figure this out, won't we? Together?"

I nodded at him and floated backward toward the privacy curtain. "Together."

Chapter Nineteen

Five Missing Mer

I left Lyssa on the schoolreef with a growing gathering of students.

Not a single teacher had arrived, but as I swam away from school, I passed Calandra in the canal, her hair bouncing up and down as she bobbed through the water.

She looked almost worried—maybe because she was late—so I hoped the enchantment was wearing off.

And that the serpent would stop singing long enough for us to execute a plan.

I dodged behind a dolphin-driven cart before Calandra could see me.

Next stop—Lyssa's house.

The canals grew a little busier. I even passed three or four dolphin-driven carts on the way. Things weren't normal yet—on a normal day, the canals would be packed—but it seemed like another good sign.

We just need a little more time ... before the serpent sings again.

As soon as I got home, I'd talk to Father and try to convince him to send out the Royal Mer Guard to fight the serpent.

I reached Lyssa's house, a large, sprawling home made of black stone and orange coral, and darted up the path. There was a coral garden on either side of the house, perfectly maintained. Lyssa's mother had always been proud of her coral garden.

The sight of the garden reassured me. I'm not sure why—I guess it was another small sign of normalcy. Though, deep down, I knew that the garden would fall into disrepair soon if we couldn't stop the singing serpent. Lyssa's mother wouldn't care about it enough to maintain it.

I knocked on the door and waited.

Nothing.

I knocked again.

Finally, the door creaked open, and Lyssa's mother appeared, floating in the doorway. She looked a little worried and a lot confused.

"Princess?" she asked, her face scrunching up. She rubbed her temples. "I'm sorry . . . I must be getting sick. My head feels so fuzzy."

"Lyssa stayed with me last night," I blurted, "she's at school. She'll be home at the normal time today."

She relaxed and rested a hand over her heart. "Oh, thank the tides. I was just thinking I couldn't remember Lyssa coming home last night or leaving for school this morning. But . . . I wasn't worried about her last night, so I must have known she was going somewhere."

"She was just with me," I said, smiling wide. "Nothing to worry about."

"Thank you, my dear." Deeper wrinkles creased her forehead. "Shouldn't you be at school, too?"

"I'm conducting royal business today," I said in my most official-sounding voice. "A higher priority than school."

She nodded slowly, though her expression suggested she thought my answer odd. The enchantment was *definitely* wearing off. I had to get home right away and talk to Father.

"Got to go!" I called, whirling around and swimming as fast as I could.

More mer crowded the canals now, and I took a shortcut down a narrow culvert between buildings.

To the palace.

A handful of dolphin-driven carts blocked my way—two on my level, near the seafloor, and two more above me. I grunted in frustration and glanced up around the carts, toward the rippling surface.

Did I dare swim higher—above the buildings—to reach the palace faster?

Mother and Father didn't like me to swim too high. Especially now, with a monster on the reef, it might not be safe.

A flash of conversation caught my attention. I tilted my head, listening to the cart drivers in front of me.

"—heard of four disappearances," said one.

My stomach sank like a rock. *Four disappearances?*

"Bad business," grunted the other. "It's all so strange."

"They're not sure when Sanna vanished," said the first. "They didn't realize she was gone until this morning. And my cousin's neighbor's son is missing too."

"Who are the others?" muttered the other merman. "This is uncanny."

The first merman grunted again. "I think a merchant, and a soldier, too. That's just hearsay, though. Or a rumor, really."

A soldier? My thoughts darted to the reef trip, when I'd first heard the song. Had a soldier gone missing, then? *Only five came back with us.* I'd thought I'd miscounted, but . . .

Quillpricks ran down my spine. I felt cold. This was getting out of control.

I darted upward, zipping around the carts until I broke into the open water above them.

Then I stopped, floating just above the buildings. I could look out over much of the city from here—and to the reef beyond. I swallowed back my fear and sadness.

Four disappearances.

I needed to get home. The Royal Mer Guard *needed* to drive away the serpent. And if they couldn't . . . then I, as the city's crown princess, needed to act. I needed to protect the people.

From the direction of the reef, the song rose up, low and mournful and frightening.

"No," I whispered, panic choking me. "It can't be happening again already! It can't be!"

My eyes swept back and forth, scanning the reef for the serpent, but I couldn't see it.

With a shiver, I glanced down at the canal beneath me.

The cart drivers gradually relaxed, falling under the enchantment. Most of the dolphins lumbered on slowly, not swimming in a straight line. One cart sank and settled against the seafloor, the driver slumped asleep in his seat.

From the corner of my eye, movement caught my attention. I watched, horrified, as an older mermaid swam over the wall, onto the reef. I couldn't see her face, though I thought she looked familiar...

She was too far away for me to catch her, but I swam after her anyway.

"Wait!" I screamed. "Don't go!"

But she didn't hear me. She just swam onward, unwavering, toward the song.

I stopped when I reached the wall and stared out after her helplessly.

Then I remembered. *The song...*

The song had been sung again, which meant Father and the soldiers would be lazy and relaxed when I went home to the palace. We wouldn't be able to convince them that the serpent was dangerous or that something needed to be done.

The mermaid vanished from sight behind distant coral. Hot determination swelled in my throat, and I grasped at a new thought.

Back in the throne room, the day I saw the monster on the reef, Lady Seraphina had said something important about serpents... something about how they hunted.

I searched my memories. Hadn't she said that serpents hunted over several days? That they kept their victims alive and ... wrapped up somewhere? In some sort of netting?

Hope washed over me.

Maybe there was still time to save the missing mer!

Protect the people. It had been the most important command Father had given me. The thing he'd said over and over again from the time I was small.

I'm the crown princess. And right now, I'm one of only three mer in this city unaffected by this siren magic.

We couldn't wait for Father and the Royal Mer Guard any longer.

The idea in my head came together all at once. But first, Nathanael and I would pay Lady Seraphina a visit.

Because it was time to put together our plan.

Chapter Twenty

Making a Plan

With a shout, I burst into the room Mother and Father shared.

Father tugged the pillow over his head and grumbled something, then resumed his bubbly snoring. Mother glanced up from her seat at their little table, near a sculpture of a dolphin. Her face looked pale, and worry lined her eyes.

"The serpent sang again?" she murmured, wringing her hands.

I nodded, biting my lip. "Yeah. And I found out something important. Where's Nathanael?"

"Here," called Nathanael as he swam through the privacy curtain, munching on a piece of fish wrapped in seaweed. "Had to get myself breakfast. The cook went back to bed as soon as he heard the song."

"I need to talk to both of you!" I exclaimed.

"Oh?" Mother raised an eyebrow.

"There have been more disappearances," I blurted. "Five total. At least."

"Five missing mer?" she gasped. "Are you sure?"

"Those are just the ones I know about. In the canal this morning, I heard a couple mermen talking about more disappearances, and . . . when the serpent sang this time, I saw a mermaid swim over the wall."

Mother crossed her arms and shot me a disapproving look. "Why were you swimming high enough to see over the wall?"

I clenched my fists at my sides. Was *that* what she was most concerned about?

"We need to do something!" I said, practically yelling. "Sitting around waiting for Father to snap out of it isn't keeping the people safe!"

"It's my job to keep *you* safe!" she snapped.

"If we don't do something, none of us will be safe!"

She held out her hands, desperate. "What are we supposed to do?"

"We need to take care of the serpent. Drive it away—or kill it, if we have to."

She scoffed. "There are only three of us, and you two are children."

"Nathanael and I have both trained to fight," I said softly.

Father rolled over in the hammock with a soft groan.

Her voice quieted, and she ran a hand through her long hair. "Well, I didn't train in combat when I was younger. I know basic self-defense, of course, but I can't wield a blade or a club. And I can't send you children out alone to face a monster we know nothing about."

She was right, I realized. She couldn't face the monster. She didn't know the first thing about handling a weapon. And she, as our mother, couldn't ask us to face the monster alone.

But it was still my duty to fight it.

Protect the people. I glanced at Father's sleeping form.

I didn't want to do this.

I didn't want to disobey Mother, and I certainly didn't want to go out onto the reef looking for the serpent. But every time I blinked, I saw that missing mermaid. Saw her swimming out toward the monster, lured by its voice.

Protect the people.

So, in a small voice, I said, "I'm going to go get some breakfast."

I stared at Nathanael, hoping he'd understand that I wanted him to come with me. An idea swirled in my head, and I needed to talk it over with him.

Nathanael swallowed the last of his fish and muttered, "I'm still hungry too."

Mother watched us with a raised eyebrow. Suspicious, no doubt. But I tried to look innocent as we swam out of the room.

"Kitchen," I hissed to Nathanael.

"That's what you said already . . ."

"Fast."

We darted down the hallway, racing.

When we careened into the kitchen, I searched the nets full of food on the center table, boasting many kinds of fish, crabs, seaweed, cucumbers. I made a face at the cucumbers.

Cucumbers were gross, slimy animals that reminded me too much of slugs. I refused to eat them.

My stomach rumbled—I really *was* hungry.

Nathanael and I each grabbed chopped pieces of fish, and I wrapped mine in a strip of seaweed. I bit into my meal with a *chomp*, chewing as I thought.

"We have to do something," I began, covering my mouth with my hand.

Nathanael nodded glumly. "I know. But what?"

"I'm putting together a plan," I said, eyeing the netting. "But I want to talk to Lady Seraphina first."

Nathanael scratched his head with his free hand. "She was the one who said something about serpents, right? You overheard her when you were eavesdropping on the throne room?"

"Yeah." I swallowed a mouthful of fish. "She'd heard bedtime stories about serpents when she was young."

He raised a skeptical eyebrow. "How much of those stories do you think are true, though?"

"Well, we don't have much else to go on, do we?" I asked. "Even Lord Dryas didn't know much about them. He only knew what they looked like." I swallowed the last of my breakfast.

Nathanael set the rest of his fish down. "I'm not sure I'm hungry anymore."

I swam back over to the long center table. "Help me with this," I said, pointing to the strip of netting beneath the pile of crabs.

He floated to the other side of the table. "Help you with what, exactly?"

I squinted at the netting. It was about as long as I was, and twice as wide. Plus, the holes were tiny, to keep the smaller crabs from falling through.

"Can we move all the crabs and take the netting?" I asked.

Nathanael looked from side to side. "We can put the crabs with the lobsters," he said, pointing to a strip of netting at the far end of the table. "There's room there."

We grabbed handfuls of crabs and swam back and forth from one end of the table to the other. When the piece of netting lay empty, I grabbed it and rolled it into a small ball.

"There," I said triumphantly.

"What's the plan?" asked Nathanael.

I glanced toward the hallway and shook my head. "Tell you in a little bit," I whispered.

We swam to the door, and I poked my head into the hallway. It was empty.

I grabbed Nathanael's arm and pulled him along, swimming in the opposite direction of Mother and Father's room.

"Let's leave the palace through the throne room," I murmured. "Just in case Lady Seraphina's there."

"Sure," said Nathanael. "Can you please tell me the plan now?"

"Once we're outside."

We reached the small door to the hallway near the throne room and found it unguarded.

Everything really had turned upside down.

We swam through it, and I peeked into the throne room. Totally empty.

My gills pulsed more quickly. I'd expected this. Expected to find no one there or just one or two advisors too befuddled to notice us.

The plan was coming off without a hitch—but the sight of the empty room, on a day when Mother and Father should be surrounded by advisors conducting royal business...

It proved how badly things had gone wrong.

We swam out of the palace. I motioned Nathanael to follow me onto one of the little paths that snaked through the coral gardens.

We arrived at my favorite anemone, and I tugged Nathanael behind it. The anemone's huge blue fringes waved softly in the water, and a pair of orange-and-white clownies swam through it.

We sank onto the seafloor, hidden from the view of anyone peering from a palace window.

"Let's find Lady Seraphina first," I said, "and try to get any information we can about the serpents."

"Will she tell us anything?" he asked, wrinkling his nose. "Or will she just glance up at us and fall asleep again?"

"Lord Dryas talked to us," I answered. "He was too tired to think straight. I think we can get answers from Lady Seraphina too."

At least, I hope so.

Nathanael shrugged and batted at the netting in my hands. "After we talk to Lady Seraphina, what's your plan?"

"We'll find out everything we can about serpents, then go to the armory and get blades and clubs," I said.

"Blades?" Nathanael asked, wide-eyed. "Real ones?"

I nodded, swallowing. "Real ones."

"Then what?" Nathanael squeaked.

"The blades are just in case," I said. "Like Artemis told us in fight training. We'll try not to use them—we don't want the serpent's blood in the water if at all possible. But I want to be prepared in case it's the only way to stop the serpent before it starts eating the missing mer."

Nathanael's jaw dropped. "Wait, you think it hasn't eaten the mer yet?"

"I'll explain on the way to see Lady Seraphina," I said, waving a hand. "First, we'll try to set a trap for it."

I held up the netting. "Remember how Artemis said that tangling a monster in netting was always a good idea? We'll find a place in the coral we can hang this net, stretching it out. Then we'll use ourselves as bait and get the serpent to chase us."

"Chase us?" Nathanael squeaked, his hand flying to his mouth.

"That's right," I said with determination. "We'll try to get it to swim straight into the netting. If we can just get the netting tied around its mouth, it won't be able to sing anymore."

Nathanael's jaw dropped. At first, he didn't say anything. Then he nodded slowly. "And everyone will wake all the way up again."

I pointed at him. "Exactly! We don't *need* to drive it away ourselves or kill it. We just need to stop it from singing long enough to get the Royal Mer Guard to understand what's going on."

Chewing his lip, Nathanael said, "I don't know, Sea Star. It seems like a lot could go wrong."

"I know." I rubbed the rough netting. "I'm nervous about it too. But we're trained how to fight—how to move quickly, how to use the environment to help us in a tight spot . . . and how to use a blade, if it comes to that. Artemis showed us those tricks for fighting monsters. Plus, I'm good at tying knots."

"This whole thing is tying *me* in knots," Nathanael muttered, scratching the side of his gill.

"I'm afraid, too," I said, catching his gaze.

We looked at each other for a long moment.

I continued, "Father says he's been afraid lots of times, you know. The trick is to do the right thing even when you're afraid."

I was saying it as much to myself as to Nathanael. Because, even with all my fight training, when I thought of that monster I'd glimpsed on the reef, terror flooded me.

And now I was going to fight it.

Chapter Twenty-One

Do It Afraid

We arrived at Lady Seraphina's coral mansion and swam straight to the front door.

I knocked politely on the smooth black stone, then floated backward, sinking until my tail brushed the seafloor.

Nothing happened. I couldn't hear any movement from inside the house.

After a moment, I knocked again. "Lady Seraphina?" I called.

No one answered.

I pounded on the door, louder. Still no answer.

Nathanael chewed his knuckle. "Maybe she doesn't want to talk."

I didn't reply. Nervousness whirlpooled in my stomach, but I *had* to speak with Lady Seraphina. She was the only one who seemed to know anything about serpents.

"Or maybe she's taking a nap because the siren enchantment made her tired," my brother added. "Do you think she'll even be able to answer our questions, or will she just be tired and confused?"

"We *need* more information," I said, steeling myself and turning back to the door with a stubborn *harrumph*.

This time, I banged as hard as I could, yelling, "Lady Seraphina!"

A rustling came from inside, and hope filled me.

Finally, the door opened, revealing Lady Seraphina's eight-year-old daughter. She blinked at us and yawned, her lava-red hair floating around her face in soft waves.

"Is your mother here?" I asked, trying to stuff down my impatience.

The girl shrugged and rubbed her eyes. "I dunno. Probably."

I bit down on the inside of my cheek. We didn't have time for delays. "Is it alright if we come in and look for her?" I asked.

She shrugged again and moved aside to let us pass. "Sure."

We floated into the house. Everything around us felt quiet. Too quiet.

Deadly quiet.

"Lady Seraphina?" I called cautiously.

No one responded.

In the distance, the first notes of music rang out. The song again. I gritted my teeth.

"Nooooo," groaned Nathanael. "Already?"

"Maybe it's really hungry," I murmured. "Maybe it's trying to get enough prey so it can eat its meal."

"Which means we're nearly out of time," finished Nathanael.

Exactly. I raised my voice, more desperate. "Lady Seraphina?"

"Useless right after the song," said Nathanael. "She's asleep for sure."

I glanced at Lady Seraphina's daughter. The girl had sunk into a hammock chair and curled up in sleep, dead to the world.

With a grunt of frustration, I declared, "We'll search the house and shake her awake, then."

I nodded toward a vertical corridor that led to the second level of the house.

"I'll look up there," I said. Then I gestured toward another hallway, this one running toward the back of the home. "You search the rooms back there."

I swam toward the vertical corridor and floated upward until I emerged in a short hallway with three doors on each side. Probably the family's sleeping chambers.

"Lady Seraphina?" I called again.

With a frown, I poked my head through a door curtain. No one occupied the first room—though the tablets and clothing strewn everywhere made me think it probably belonged to the little girl.

The second room was even emptier—with no one there, and mostly empty of things, too. It just had a hammock and a table and a wardrobe, all perfectly tidy.

Perhaps this is a guest room.

When I peeked into the third chamber, I darted backward, startled. A large merman was asleep in a hammock bed. My gills opened and closed quickly as I calmed myself.

Just Lady Seraphina's husband. This must be their room.

With a flash of determination, I peeked in again, looking for Lady Seraphina. The big merman rolled over and grunted, but there was no one else in the hammock, or anywhere.

I backed away and peeked into the three remaining rooms. No one else was up here.

Maybe Nathanael had found Lady Seraphina below. I swam back to the first level.

The girl still slept in the hammock chair, and Nathanael was just returning from the back hallway.

"Is she up there?" he asked.

I furrowed my brow. "Nope. Not down here, either?"

"Maybe she went to the throne room," he said, pointing at an ornate tide glass, decorated with pearls. "Maybe she was on her way there while we were on our way here, and she took a different canal."

"No telling where she might have gone, with the state everything is in . . ." Then I froze, my thoughts flashing back to what I'd seen that morning.

The mermaid who swam over the city wall. Could it be? "Oh no," I whispered.

"What is it?" Nathanael asked.

I hurried to the girl's side and shook her.

She groaned and slapped at my hand, but I shook her again. Her eyes cracked open, and she squinted at me.

"What is it?" she muttered.

"Your mother," I said, "did she leave this morning?"

The girl blinked. "I . . . don't remember."

"Think!" I clapped my hands in front of her face. "Think as hard as you can."

She stretched to her full length—which was still quite short—then tilted her head.

"Yeah . . ." she said finally. "The music. She was reading, but then she wanted to see the music, I guess. I was too sleepy to go. Still sleepy." She gave a cavernous yawn.

Nathanael squeaked, "The music?"

I put a finger to my lips to warn him to be quiet. We didn't want to scare Lady Seraphina's daughter.

Although, I thought as the girl curled back up into a ball and went to sleep, *with this enchantment, there's little fear of scaring anyone.*

"Let's go," I said. Nathanael followed me out of the house, and I closed the door behind us.

We hovered a moment in silence, staring at each other. Nathanael pressed his fist against his mouth.

"It was her," I said finally. "The mermaid I saw leave the city. It was Lady Seraphina. I only saw her from behind, and I thought she looked familiar. I couldn't place her. But now . . ."

"The monster ate her?" asked Nathanael, his jaw dropping. He clamped his mouth shut, gnawing on his pointer finger.

The thought made me sick to my stomach. "I . . . hope not," I said. "I hope she's just wrapped up, and that the serpent hasn't eaten anyone yet."

"You're sure we can save them?" he asked. "All of them?"

I hesitated. "Well . . . at least I hope so."

He squared his shoulders and pointed his chin upward. "Then we have to try."

I reached out, and we clasped forearms. Somehow, the formal gesture felt right, with what we were about to do.

"To protect the people?" I asked with a sad smile.

He nodded firmly. "Somehow."

"If we can't learn more about the serpent," I said, "we need to make sure the plan is solid. We might only have one chance at this."

And if we're not careful, we might get wrapped up for dinner too.

"Well, let's go to the armory now," he said. "This is the best time, right after the song. The armory guards will be sound asleep, or at least they won't care we're there."

"Good point," I said, reaching out and slapping my hand against his.

He grabbed my hand and squeezed it tight. "Do it afraid? Like Father says?"

I managed a tight smile. "Yeah. We'll do it afraid."

Chapter Twenty-two

Lyssa Lost

On the way to the armory, Nathanael and I hurtled down Grand Canal, past shops and restaurants that were quieter than I'd ever seen them.

The stillness hovered around us, eerie and frightening. Usually, mer swam on Grand Canal at all hours of day and night—and this time of day, it should be packed.

But now?

A few mer milled aimlessly, floating halfheartedly toward their destinations in a daze. Others slept in doorways or on carts. A few had sunk to the seafloor in the middle of the canal, slumbering in the swimway.

"I hate this," Nathanael muttered.

"Me too." Quillpricks shuddered down my spine, and I hugged myself. Looking around at the dazed and sleeping mer made me queasy. This wasn't right.

Then the song started again, the tones low and haunting. I clenched my fists, and the netting I was carrying dug into my skin.

"No!" I groaned. "Stop it!"

Nathanael covered his ears. "Why does it keep happening?" he yelled. "It's singing over and over again! Before, it went a long time between songs."

I didn't know the answer for sure. But I did know that, this morning, the song had lured Lady Seraphina out of her house and onto the reef.

We'd nearly reached the armory, but a terrible thought struck me.

Which must mean that, right now ... the serpent is luring someone out of the city!

I darted upward, toward the silvery surface. I stopped over a nearby rooftop, floating high enough to overlook the whole city—to watch for mer swimming out onto the reef.

"Oh no," I whispered.

A girl about my age was swimming over the city wall. She had magenta hair and a white tail just like . . .

Panic exploded in my whole body. I dropped the netting, and it sank toward the rooftop.

No. No, no, no, no.

It wasn't. It couldn't be!

"Lyssa!" I shrieked.

Abandoning all thoughts of the armory and swimming as fast as I could toward my friend, I screamed, "Lyssa! Stop!"

But just like Lady Seraphina, Lyssa acted like she didn't even hear me. She just kept swimming. She crossed the wall, leaving the city.

She's on the reef!

I heaved, my body tingling, panic dulling my senses.

Why her? Why Lyssa?

A dull ache in my chest told me I shouldn't have been surprised. Lyssa had been drawn to the song, to the serpent, from the beginning.

But I wouldn't let the serpent have her.

"Stop, Lyssa!" I yelled.

I felt a tug on my fin, but I shook it away. Then the tug came again, sharper. Pain shot up my tail. I whirled on Nathanael.

"It's Lyssa," I sputtered. "We have to help her. We have to bring her back!"

Fear pounded so loudly in my ears that I couldn't hear my brother's words. He gestured toward the armory.

"We have to get her!" I yelled, ripping myself away and swimming after Lyssa.

I could sense Nathanael following me. He was still trying to say something, but I couldn't think of anything except saving Lyssa.

In the distance, light glinted off her white tail.

There was still time. We could bring her back.

Nathanael grabbed my arm. "We need to get the weapons," he said. "We'll have a better chance of saving her that way."

"I can still see her," I spat. "I'm not going to leave her to get caught by the monster. We can bring her back." With a lurch forward, I swam even faster.

Beneath me, the reef seemed to blur. The fish were swimming like usual—perhaps a little lazier than normal.

The song must affect them too. They don't realize there's a monster nearby.

"Lyssa!" I yelled again.

Now I could see her hair streaming behind her. We were gaining on her.

A blur of motion intruded on my vision. A long, thin shape shot through the water toward Lyssa.

"Nooooo!" I screamed.

The monster curled itself around Lyssa and dragged her away, off ahead and to my right.

I kept swimming.

I wasn't afraid now. Not anymore. The serpent had my best friend. I wouldn't stop until I got her back.

Nathanael grabbed my arm again. "Let's follow it," he said. "Figure out what it's doing and where its lair is. If it's just wrapping everyone up, and they're all alive, we need to go back for weapons before we fight it."

"Fine," I snapped. "I'm going to get her home safe."

"*You* said we needed to make sure our plan was solid," he muttered.

"It's Lyssa!" A sob choked off my words. The serpent was slicing through the water fast. I put all my effort into keeping it in sight. Ahead, I spotted the entrance to a cave, a small opening in a wall of rock.

The monster eased inside, taking Lyssa with it. My best friend vanished into the mouth of the cave.

My heart pounded faster.

"Now we know where its lair is," said Nathanael. "That's good. That'll help us. Let's look for seamarks so we can find this place again."

"I'm going in to get her," I said stubbornly.

After a brief hesitation, he said, "We'll scout it out, but . . . Sea Star? We need to be smart about this."

I knew he was right, but . . . "If it were Cyrus, you'd be charging in there ahead of me," I pointed out.

He grabbed my face with both his hands and made me look at him.

"You're probably right," he said. "But that doesn't mean it'd be smart. We have a better chance at getting her out of there if we're smart about it. If it were Cyrus, you'd be the one holding me back and telling me to think this through." He let me go, and I jerked my attention back to the cave. The end of the serpent's tail disappeared inside, curling like seaweed on a current.

"Let's go," I said. "We'll scout it out, like you said. I'll be smart."

Probably.

We crept forward until we reached the mouth of the cave.

"I'll go first," I whispered. I needed to keep my best friend safe, but I wanted to protect my little brother too.

I reached forward and brushed either side of the cave wall. It was narrow, with only enough room to swim single file. Which made it a perfect hiding place for a monster like the serpent.

A webbed-foot dragon or a great shark couldn't use this cave—the entrance is too narrow.

I swam forward, stretching my hands in front of me. The light dimmed into darkness, and my gills flared. We were swimming into a monster's lair, and I couldn't see past my fingertips.

Maybe Nathanael was right. Maybe we were going into this foolishly. But what if this cave branched out in many directions and we lost our chance to find Lyssa by delaying? I swallowed back the fear and swam forward.

Do it afraid.

My fingers skimmed against the close stone walls.

"How far do you think we'll have to swim?" Nathanael whispered.

"I don't know."

But it wasn't long before the stone fell away beneath my fingers. I pulled to an abrupt stop.

Nathanael crashed into my back but didn't say anything. We waited, listening, staying perfectly still. After a moment, I gently pulled him forward. A stream of light shone through the tunnel behind us.

We mer needed only a few pinpricks of light. If we waited, our eyes would adjust to the darkness, and we'd be able to see.

In the meantime, I focused on my surroundings, tried to *feel* them. I sensed the cavern was big, opening up around us like a gaping mouth. I shivered.

Plankton by plankton, my eyes adjusted, and I made out movement . . . then shapes. We floated in a giant, round cavern. Eight or ten bundles were attached to the walls, spaced out from each other at uneven intervals. The bundles reminded me of the shoal-moth cocoons Quirinia had shown us a couple years earlier. I hadn't been to the rocky shallows near the shore, where shoal-moth larvae spun underwater cocoons to transform themselves into full-fledged moths before climbing up the rocks and flying away. But I remembered the lesson well, and these bundles reminded me of the cocoons.

I squinted at the nearest bundle. Then I glimpsed the serpent, on the far side of the cavern.

"Stay here," I whispered in Nathanael's ear.

I crept along the wall until I reached the bundle. A fin stuck out from the bottom. I dug my nails into my palms.

Then I saw her face—a mermaid, body wrapped in some sort of silvery-black cloth.

Lady Seraphina!

Her head tilted forward and her eyes had fluttered closed, but her gills moved steadily, inhaling and exhaling water.

She's still alive!

I tugged at the black cloth, and part of it pulled away in my hand. It felt like the cloth was made of small, sticky strands.

My forehead wrinkled. That didn't make sense.

Was this the strange netting Lady Seraphina had mentioned?

I glanced back over at the serpent. It hadn't seemed to detect our presence yet—or maybe it didn't care. Maybe it thought of us as just another kind of fish.

My fingers brushed something hard. I squinted, reaching out to trace the shape. *A tablet?*

Lady Seraphina was holding a stone tablet.

I tore away a few of the threads around the tablet. They clung to my hand, and I wiped them away on the stone wall.

Gross.

Tugging out the tablet proved harder than I'd anticipated.

It'll be nearly impossible to free all these mer with just our hands, I realized in despair. *Even if we get the serpent to leave the lair.*

Finally, I extricated the tablet, detecting faint scrib markings on its surface—but the cavern didn't have enough light to read by. With a shudder, I wiped the remaining strands off my hands.

Then my eyes landed on Lyssa.

She was floating, the serpent swimming around and around her. I could just make out silvery-black strands shooting from the back of the serpent's tail.

It was making the strange cloth and wrapping Lyssa up!

I glanced down at Lady Seraphina again, my stomach churning like a storm.

She's alive, I reminded myself. *For now.*

I'd promised Nathanael I'd be smart. And based on how hard it had been to get Lady Seraphina's tablet, we couldn't free the mer right away.

We needed tools to cut through the webbing.

Everything in me ached at what I was about to do.

How could I leave my best friend to be wrapped up like a fish in seaweed?

But I glided back to Nathanael, moving silently through the water. He was right. This time.

We stood a better chance at saving the missing mer if we returned with blades. This room was too open and empty, and the serpent swam fast.

It'd be hard enough to fight it in here—especially without any weapons. Too much of a risk of getting caught ourselves—and we couldn't help Lyssa if we got wrapped up in those threads.

I shoved Nathanael toward the tunnel, and we swam as quickly as we could through the narrow space.

When we burst back out onto the reef, Nathanael whirled to face me, clenching his hands.

"Armory?" I asked.

He gestured toward the tablet in my hand. "What's that?"

"Lady Seraphina had it with her," I said. "I . . . thought it might be important."

Swish. A soft noise came from inside the cave.

I startled, flipping away from the entrance. Was the serpent darting toward us, through the long, narrow tunnel?

"Swim!" I pointed at the city. "We can't get caught by that thing. We'll come back with blades."

Chapter Twenty-Three
Seven Hunts

My heartbeat slowed as we reached the city wall.

I spared a final glance backward—no sign of the monster. Maybe it hadn't been following us.

Or maybe it was good at sneaking around the reef unseen.

"How about here?" I asked, pointing at a section of wall that looked abandoned.

We swam upward, skimming as close as we could to the wall, then dropped down into the city, finding ourselves in an abandoned culvert behind a row of shops.

Nathanael's face looked ashen, and his gills pulsed harder than usual. He tapped Lady Seraphina's tablet and croaked, "What does it say? Is it important?"

I leaned against the barnacle-covered wall and began to read, "On the subject of serpents," I said slowly.

I looked up at Nathanael, eyes wide. "Look at this insignia in the top corner! This isn't one of Lady Seraphina's personal tablets—she found this in the royal library!"

"Whoa!" He snatched it out of my hand. "No one's allowed to take tablets out of the library."

I grabbed it back. "But no one's concerned about the rules when they're enchanted by the serpent's song. She must have been in the library, doing research, when she heard the serpent sing, and she didn't bother to set down the tablet in her hand."

He scrunched up his face. "But didn't Lady Seraphina leave early in the morning? From her house?"

He was right—I'd seen Lady Seraphina leave in the morning.

And her daughter had said that she'd been reading . . . and then gone to see the music.

"She must have taken the tablet from the library against the rules, then," I said. "Maybe when the serpent sang another time—or maybe, when the earlier song started wearing off, she realized something was terribly wrong with the city, and she was willing to break a rule to help figure it out."

"I mean, we've broken a lot of rules today," muttered Nathanael.

I stared at the tablet. "Lady Seraphina thought the serpent had something to do with it—with everyone acting bewitched. It must have taken her a while to even find this tablet—hardly anyone in Thessalonike has heard of serpents."

Nathanael poked my arm. "Well, what does the tablet say?"

I read, "One of the great monsters of the deep, the serpent uses stealth and cunning to hunt its prey. Unlike most animals, the serpent does not feed every day. It goes for months without eating. When it feels hunger, it begins seven hunts, carrying off prey in ones or twos or threes to its lair and wrapping it in webbing it spins from its tail."

My eyes widened, and I jolted up to face Nathanael. "This tablet is exactly right!" I exclaimed. "That weird netting came out of the serpent's tail. Whoever wrote this really knew about serpents! They weren't just repeating legends!"

"But this serpent isn't hunting by stealth," Nathanael pointed out, scraping at a barnacle. "It's luring mer in with its song."

"But we think sirens enchanted *this* serpent, using the magic they stole from Mother's childhood city! Oh, and look here!" I pointed at a line in the middle of the tablet.

I continued, "Serpents can live over a hundred years. So, the sirens could have enchanted the serpent years and years ago, when Mother was a child. Now it's escaped, but it still has siren song. It's figured out it's easier to hunt by singing than by stealth."

Nathanael fidgeted with his hands, considering this idea. "That makes sense," he finally said. "I think you're right." Then he bit his lip. "Um . . . Sea Star?"

"What?"

"Read the sentence about how serpents hunt again."

I looked down at the tablet. "One of the great monsters—"

"Sorry, no." He waved a hand impatiently. "The next one."

I cleared my throat. "Unlike most animals, the serpent does not feed every day."

"Keep going." He clasped his hands until his knuckles turned white.

"It goes for months without eating. When it feels hunger, it begins seven hunts, carrying off prey to its lair in ones or twos or threes and wrapping it—"

"That's it!" exclaimed Nathanael. "Seven hunts! And it can wrap up three mer with each hunt! So there will be somewhere between seven and"—he paused and tilted his head, multiplying—"between seven and twenty-one captured mer! What happens after the seventh hunt, Sea Star?"

With a sick feeling in my stomach, I leaned forward. "When it feels hunger, it begins seven hunts, carrying off prey to its lair in ones or twos or threes and wrapping it in webbing it spins from its tail. Between each hunt, it rests, regaining its strength. The length of time between each hunt reflects the depth of its hunger. After the seventh hunt, it feasts on its captured prey."

Dizziness gripped me, the lines of writing wavering.

Nathanael's voice took on a more urgent tone. "How many times has the serpent sung?"

"Well," I said tremulously. "I heard it once on the reef."

"Then it woke you up in the middle of the night, what—a day and a half later?" He held up two fingers.

"That's right." I ran a hand through my long hair. "And a third time—that afternoon, when Lyssa was in my room."

"It sang a fourth time"—he ticked up a fourth finger for emphasis—"the morning after that, right before we were going to explain the enchantment to Father."

"When Lady Seraphina followed the song," I added.

"Whoa! That was *this* morning, wasn't it?" he almost yelled.

I rubbed my temples. This was making my head hurt. "Guess so. And then . . ."

I trailed off. I couldn't talk about the fifth song. It hurt too much.

Nathanael held up five fingers. "Then the fifth time was right before we followed Lyssa out onto the reef, at about midday."

I nodded, following along with his stream of thought. "Which means, if the serpent hunts seven times, it's only going to sing twice more before . . . before it's too late."

"And," he squeaked, "the tablet said that the time between the hunts reflects how hungry it is. It must be getting hungrier and hungrier, because the time between the songs has gotten shorter and shorter. It won't get any *less* hungry before it feeds. It will only get *hungrier*. At this rate . . ."

My arms and fin felt heavy as I calculated in my head, "At this rate, it will sing once this afternoon."

"The sixth song." He clenched his hands into fists.

"And by evening . . ." I gripped the tablet tighter. Terror shot through my limbs.

My brother and I stared at each other, pausing for a long moment.

In unison, we blurted, "The seventh song."

Chapter Twenty-Four

A Detour

"We don't have much time!" I exclaimed, shoving off the barnacle-covered wall. "Quickly!"

As we sliced through the water, I whispered, "I'm coming, Lyssa."

We have enough time to save everyone, I told myself. *As long as nothing else goes wrong.*

"Okay," Nathanael called as we careened around the corner onto a wide canal. "We're going to the armory next, right?"

"Yeah," I yelled. "I dropped our netting there. We'll pick that up and find ourselves some good blades."

Kicking our tails, we surged forward, around another corner, past a group of mer in lazy conversation, past a school of blue-and-green fish, past the new sculpture garden in the center of the city.

"That way," I said as the armory came into view. I pointed left, toward a subdued sandstone building that didn't draw attention to itself.

"Almost there," whispered Nathanael. "Let's slow down so we won't look suspicious."

Not that it matters much, I thought glumly as I looked up and down the nearly empty canal. *There's hardly anyone here to see us.*

But I slowed to a leisurely pace, just in case.

One soldier floated outside the armory door, staring across the canal . . . at a plain brown wall.

"I don't think he's going to give us much trouble," I murmured.

"Do we just swim past him?" asked Nathanael, nudging me.

"Does he look like he's going to stop us?" I replied, squinting at the entranced soldier. "The trick is to be confident. To not give him any reason to think we're not supposed to be here. And hope that the song's enchantment confuses him enough that he doesn't challenge us."

"Good point," muttered Nathanael.

We approached the door and slipped behind the soldier. He turned to face us, but his movements were sluggish.

"What . . . are you doing?" the soldier asked. He scratched the bridge of his nose.

"Official royal business," I said firmly, continuing toward the door.

"No," he said slowly, blinking hard. "You're too young. You're the princess and prince. You . . . don't come here."

What terrible tides. I bit the inside of my cheek. Of course we'd found the *one* guard in the city so good at his job that even siren enchantment couldn't overcome all his common sense.

Despite my frustration, I admired him for not completely succumbing to the magic. He was a good soldier. A *great* soldier.

For an extra heartbeat, I studied him so I could describe him to Father later, after we'd saved the city and everyone woke up from their stupor. This soldier should be an officer in the Royal Mer Guard, not a mere sentry.

But right now I *needed* to get Lyssa—and all the other mer—out of that cave. Should we assure the soldier that everything was fine? Or appeal to his deeper good sense?

Deciding on the second course of action, I said, "You're right—I'm Crown Princess Eliana Hannapola, and this is Prince Nathanael Demetriopolis. Have you . . . noticed how odd everything has been recently?"

Nathanael tugged on my wrap, but I ignored him.

The soldier's lips twisted in a thoughtful expression. "Odd..." His eyes flashed back and forth between tired relaxation and alert concern.

"Yes, odd," I said as patiently as I could. But the picture of Lyssa wrapped up in those threads intruded on my mind. We didn't have time for things to go wrong. "You must have noticed. You're very serious about your job."

He nodded, and the furrow between his eyebrows deepened.

"The prince and I are here to help everything go back to normal. To protect the people and keep the city safe."

Again, he nodded. His gaze grew distant as the enchantment won the battle in his mind—for now, at least. He stared across the canal at the plain brown wall.

"Let's go," I whispered to Nathanael, pushing at the armory door. But it didn't move. *Locked. Of course it's locked.*

I bit my lip and turned back to the guard. No ring of keys hung from his belt, but I asked, "Do you happen to have the key to the armory?"

He slapped the side of his head as if trying to clear his mind again.

"Key..." he mumbled. "No. Captain Paulos has the keys." Then he looked up and down the canal. "Where *is* Captain Paulos?"

There *should* be a group of at least six soldiers stationed at the armory, but the others hadn't reported for duty. I clenched my fists.

How could we get in without the key?

"Do you know where any of the keys are right now?" Nathanael asked.

He yawned and shook his head. "No keys right now," he slurred.

Nathanael poked my arm and whispered, "This isn't working. We need another way in."

"Thank you for your service," I said to the soldier with a quick nod. Then I swam upward, beckoning Nathanael to follow.

When we reached the top of the sandstone building, I sank down to sit on the roof.

"Let's think," I said.

"No way to get through the door without a key." Nathanael sat beside me, our tails dangling off the edge.

"And no key anywhere nearby," I muttered. "But maybe there's another way in. Through a window?"

"No way." His lips pursed, and he looked like Mother. "The armory is too important. They couldn't leave any spaces open for mer to sneak in and steal things."

But I flipped my fin and launched off the roof, propelling myself toward the far end of the building. "Well, let's just look."

I reached the other side. The city stretched out before me, that unsettling stillness hovering over everything.

If we couldn't get into the armory . . . we'd have to arm ourselves with kitchen knives or something. Because we had to get back to that cave—quick.

I swam toward the seafloor, along the armory's outer wall, searching for any breaks in the sandstone. No windows anywhere on this side. I curved around the corner, turning right.

"Nathanael!" I cried in excitement.

"What?" He careened around the corner after me, colliding with my back.

I grunted, but gestured ahead—at a small window blocked by vertical bars. Even without any bars, the opening was too small for a full-grown mer to swim through. But if we could somehow get rid of the bars, Nathanael and I could barely squeeze inside.

"Whoa!" he whispered.

I darted forward and tugged wildly on the bars. They stayed planted in the sandstone, unmovable.

Scowling, I peered through the opening. Sure enough, there it was—the armory, full of weapons of every kind. Swords of different lengths, batons, clubs, spears . . . even some weapons I didn't recognize.

This room held everything we needed to defeat the serpent.

We just have to get in.

"It's sandstone," said Nathanael, peeking over my shoulder. I startled, surprised to find him so close.

"What's your point?" I asked, impatient.

"*Sandstone* is my point!" He flailed his hands. "Quirinia taught us about rocks this year."

I reached out and rested my hand on the wall. "I know it's sandstone. What does that mean?"

I should have paid more attention to rocks in Quirinia's class. I had a good head for numbers and reading and fighting, but rocks . . . not my favorite.

"It's a soft kind of rock!" he exclaimed. "We just need a harder rock to dig at it with, and it'll crumble."

His full meaning hit me with the force of a club. "If we chisel away at the rock, we can pull the bars out," I whispered.

He made a face at the tiny window. "Unless the bars are too long. They might go so deep into the stone that we can't carve them out."

I shook my head quickly. "You said it's soft rock. Is it fragile? Will it break into pieces easily?"

"Yeah, why?"

"Then they'd have to be careful putting the bars in, wouldn't they? The longer the bars, the higher chance that they'd break the whole wall apart while putting the bars in. I'm sure we can break through."

Understanding dawned on his face.

I grabbed his arm. "Let's pay Lord Dryas and his carving tools a visit."

Chapter Twenty-Five

A Seahorse Key

Nathanael and I burst into Lord Dryas's workshop without knocking. I stopped abruptly, my gaze sweeping over the room.

Lord Dryas sat slumped over his table, his back toward us. Carvings lay strewn in front of him, and a few tablets perched precariously on the edge of the table. His gills rose and fell in deep, even pulses, letting out bubbling snores.

Where are the tools?

I spotted a tiny gouge next to his hand, but that wouldn't work. We needed tools that could quickly chisel away at the sandstone.

Lyssa's life depended on it.

There. My gaze landed on a little stone chest at Lord Dryas's fin. A huge lock dangled off the front of the chest.

"I bet he keeps his sharpest tools in there," I whispered, pointing.

A familiar note of music floated to my ears, and horror swept over me.

"No!" I whispered. *It can't be.*

But the melody stubbornly drifted through the water, no matter how much I wanted it to fall quiet. The serpent was singing, already calling another mer out of the city.

"Not again," Nathanael moaned. "That wasn't enough time! It's too soon!"

"The sixth song," I said, my stomach sinking to the seafloor.

"We only have one more song before it starts eating the mer!" He clapped his hand over his mouth in horror.

We locked eyes.

"Hurry." I darted forward, ducking under the table and tugging the chest toward me. "Too heavy," I grunted.

I reached for the lock, inspecting it, trying to avoid brushing against Lord Dryas's fin. Then I glanced back at Nathanael. "The key that unlocks this chest is pretty big. It's got to be around here somewhere."

Lord Dryas twitched, and I froze. But after a brief spasm, he fell still. I tried to remind myself that the song would keep him nice and calm, even if he woke up.

He won't get angry even if he catches us in here. He'll just be confused and tired.

Nathanael swam around the room, searching along the floor, in the netting bags hanging on the hooks near the door, and on the two small tables along the wall.

"I don't see a key," he said, pursing his lips.

An idea took hold of me. "Let's check Lord Dryas. Could he be wearing the key? On his neck or around his waist?"

"Good idea!" exclaimed Nathanael.

I swam out from beneath the table. Lord Dryas wasn't wearing a cord around his waist, but . . .

"Look at that!" I pointed at a cord hanging from his neck, trailing beneath his wrap. Slowly, heart pounding, I reached out and pinched the cord. Then I tugged upward, just a little.

There was definitely something heavy hanging on the cord.

"I think I found it," I hissed.

Nathanael darted to my side and poked my arm. "How are we going to get it off him?"

"Good question." I wrinkled my nose, studying the problem. We couldn't just lift it over Lord Dryas's head—not when he was leaning forward, with his forehead against the table. And the cord looked to be a single piece of thickly woven cloth, so there was no untying it.

The serpent had just sung, weaving a new enchantment on the city—we could probably wake Lord Dryas and ask for the key ... but that posed the risk of more delays.

And when the serpent sang again ...

"We'll have to cut the cord off so we can take the key," I said.

Nathanael's eyes widened. "That's stealing!"

I glared at him and pointed down at the chest. "We came here to steal his tools."

"To *borrow* them."

"Without asking."

Nathanael just frowned.

"Point is, we don't *want* to do any of this." My throat felt tight, and the next words came out choked. "And we're going to be in an ocean of trouble when everyone wakes up, probably. But I'd rather be in an ocean of trouble and get Lyssa home safely." I'd accept whatever punishment Mother and Father gave me as long as Lyssa was home.

I leaned forward and plucked a small knife, its blade no longer than my finger, off the table. Then I swam behind Lord Dryas and motioned for Nathanael's help.

"Hold the cord on both sides," I said.

Nathanael obeyed, although he kept glancing toward the door.

As if anyone's going to come investigate what we're doing, I thought, rolling my eyes. The whole city was probably asleep.

I'm coming, Lyssa. I'm going to get you out of there.

Gently, I sawed at the cord, careful not to nick Lord Dryas. "Don't let the key fall," I warned as I cut through the last thread.

He lifted the cord until a dark gray key emerged from Lord Dryas's wrap. It was almost as big as my hand, with an intricate handle in the shape of a seahorse.

"Perfect," I whispered. The end of the key looked like a perfect fit for the lock on the chest. My gills flared as I slipped the key off the cord and held it up triumphantly.

"Let's do this," I said. I swam toward the chest.

I inserted the key in the lock and turned it. Nothing happened. I felt lightheaded. Had we guessed wrong? Would the key not work?

I turned it harder. The lock clicked, and my shoulders relaxed. *Success!*

With deliberate movements, I cracked open the chest.

A slow smile spread across my face. Just as I'd hoped—the chest held the tools we needed. I studied the selection of chisels, mallets, scrapers, gouges, and carving knives.

What will work best to get the bars out of the sandstone? Slowly and carefully, I selected two scrapers and two chisels. Above me, at Lord Dryas's table, Nathanael squeaked something I couldn't understand.

I ignored him.

"Do you think these will work for scraping sandstone?" I asked. I started to swim toward my brother, but he ducked under the table and shushed me.

"What?" I whispered.

Then a familiar voice called, "Lord Dryas?"

And I froze, crouched beneath the table with Nathanael, hiding behind Lord Dryas's feathery fin.

Because Mother hovered in the doorway.

Chapter Twenty-Six

THE SEVENTH SONG

No, no, no. Mother couldn't find us. Not yet.

She'd try to stop us from helping Lyssa. The serpent could sing the seventh song at any moment!

I tried to calm the pulsing of my gills, to stay as still as possible so she wouldn't spot us.

"Lord Dryas?" Mother called again. From our spot beneath the table, I watched Mother swim into the workshop.

She reached the table, her fin brushing the floor so close I could have touched it.

"Did she see us?" I mouthed to Nathanael.

He shook his head ever so slightly.

"Lord Dryas!" Mother practically yelled.

The story carver grunted in response and sat up. "Huh?"

From this angle, I couldn't see their faces. I dug my fingernails into my palms.

Would Lord Dryas notice that his key was missing? Would he reach for his tool chest and see us?

"Oh," he said lazily. "Your Majesty. What a p-puhleasant surprooooze."

I locked eyes with Nathanael, trying not to laugh at the absurdity.

"Lord Dryas," Mother said in a clipped voice. "I need to ask you about some old stories."

"F'course, Majestyyyyyy," he drawled.

After a brief pause, she said, "Do you know of any stories about serpents?"

He gave a long yawn. "Sssssserpentssss?" he asked. "Funny."

"What? Why would you find that funny?" Mother demanded, thrashing her fin against the floor. She rarely sounded this impatient.

"Yoooooour childers were here before." He yawned again, and his voice became a little clearer. "Asking about serpents too."

"My ... childers?" she asked, her accent thickening. Then his meaning seemed to hit her. "Ah, yes. Eliana and

Nathanael came to talk to you. They mentioned that. What did you tell them?"

Nathanael and I stared at each other. I pressed my elbows against my ribs, making myself as small as possible.

Lord Dryas's fin twitched, and Nathanael jerked back, just out of reach. I held completely still. *Did Mother feel the water move?*

But she didn't seem to notice.

After a moment, Lord Dryas said, "Drew 'em a picture of a serpent. Told 'em serpents are rare and might not even exist any"—he hiccupped—"more. I've never met anyone who's seen one. Don't know much about 'em."

She didn't respond. I imagined her forehead creasing in concern, her lips pursing in that way that meant she was worried.

"And they just came once?" she asked.

Something thumped above us—Lord Dryas's head falling forward onto the table again, I suspected.

Mother hovered next to the table for what felt like forever. I pressed my elbows even closer against my sides, willing her to leave the workshop.

Finally, she floated away. She paused in the doorway, as if thinking, then dove forward, soaring out of sight.

I slumped backward and pressed my hands against the floor, relieved. Nathanael sagged against the table leg.

A bubbly snore broke the silence, and I covered my mouth to keep from bursting into nervous laughter.

What a close call!

Nathanael whispered, "Should we go?"

"Soon," I replied. "Let's give her a head start. If she sees us in the canals, she'll try to stop us."

"She knows something's up." Nathanael rested his chin in his hands. "That we're planning something. When this is all over, she's going to lock us in the palace for the rest of our lives."

"Probably," I quipped. "What are you going to miss most about the outside world?"

"Definitely not school," he said with a half-grin. "Who needs school if you're a pampered prisoner?"

Lord Dryas snorted, and I put a finger to my lips to warn Nathanael to speak more quietly. Then I inched forward, scooted out from under the table, and floated toward the doorway.

My hands tingled as I gripped the tools. When I reached the door, I peeked out onto the canal.

"All clear," I said, turning and swimming straight into my brother. We collided, and one of the chisels scraped his arm.

"Youch!" he hissed, grabbing at his arm. "Sea Star! What'd you do that for?"

Oh no! "Why'd you come up right behind me like that?" I scowled. "You're not bleeding, are you?"

I gently pulled his fingers away from the wound and murmured, "Uh-oh."

A thin line of blood streamed out of the wound, tinging the water pink.

He bit down on his knuckles. "What are we going to do, Sea Star? I can't go out on the reef bleeding!"

I set down three of the tools and pointed a chisel at Nathanael. "Give me the very end of your wrap. We'll use it as a bandage to staunch the wound."

Nodding, he untied the end of his wrap near his belly button and held out a length of fabric to me.

"Swim closer to the wall," I said, holding up the chisel.

He obeyed. I pressed the fabric up against the stone wall, then made a sawing motion with the chisel.

At first, the fabric held strong. Panic turned in my stomach, making me feel sick. But then, a few threads tore. *This is going to work!* I kept sawing.

Though the cloth was thinning, my patience evaporated quickly.

After a few more sawing motions, I dropped the chisel, grabbed the end of the wrap in my hands, and tugged at it. The fabric tore in two, and I held up the smaller piece in triumph.

"Hold out your arm," I said to my brother.

He retied the end of his wrap, then gave me his arm. I carefully tied the cloth around the wound, watching his face out of the corner of my eye. He was uncharacteristically quiet.

When I finished tying the bandage, I said, "I'm sorry I scraped you."

"It wasn't your fault." He slumped forward.

"What's wrong?" I asked, concerned.

"I made a mistake when I came up behind you like that." He sank down to the floor and picked up the scattered tools. "I should have realized I'd startle you, and I should have thought about the sharp edges of the scrapers and the chisel. Is . . . is the serpent going to smell us coming now? Are we going to lose our chance to save everyone?"

I brushed his bandage. "I should have been more aware of my surroundings," I said firmly. "I wasn't paying attention to where you were. That sort of mistake could cost us when we're battling the serpent."

He opened his mouth, but I held up a hand to quiet him.

"We're going to defeat the serpent." I crossed my arms, realizing that I was talking more to myself than to Nathanael. Fear churned in my stomach, eating away at my insides.

Why am I so afraid?

Wasn't it normal to be afraid before doing something like this? I could get hurt, or even die.

But that's not it. That's not what I'm afraid of.

I clenched my hands as the reality hit me: *I'm afraid of failing everyone.*

Not only was I the crown princess—until the siren enchantment wore off, I was undoubtedly the city's best fighter. The serpent's song had dulled everyone else's senses and lulled them into laziness. They were just too relaxed to fight.

That's a lot of responsibility.

As I looked into my brother's eyes, the fear thickened in my throat. Was I ready to take this on? It *was* my fault that I'd scraped Nathanael's arm—what a terrible mistake!

"Sea Star?" he asked uncertainly.

"This is what we've been preparing for our whole lives," I squeaked.

At the table behind us, Lord Dryas snorted.

"Let's go," I whispered, beckoning my brother to follow me.

We peeked out onto the canal again, then swam out of the workshop.

"Back to the armory?" he asked, handing me a chisel and a scraper.

This has to work.

"Back to the armory!" I cried, trying to sound more confident than I felt. "We're going to break in, get the weapons, find the netting—"

"Where *is* the netting?" Nathanael flicked his tail to propel himself forward.

I matched his pace. "On a rooftop next to the armory. I dropped it when Lyssa . . ."

We rounded a corner onto a wider canal, and he gave a determined nod. "So, break in, get the weapons, find the netting, and swim out to the reef."

"It's a plan," I said. So, why did I feel so sick to my stomach?

When we'd nearly reached the armory, I said, "How about I get the netting while you start breaking in?"

"Meet me at the armory window," he replied.

With one final glance at the nearly empty canal, I hurtled upward, toward the rooftops. The city spread out beneath me, and my heart caught in my throat.

Thessalonike. My home.

I loved this place, and the mer in it. I turned, glimpsing the palace's teal-and-pink coral spires, about a dozen canals away.

New resolve tingled through me.

I couldn't think about whether I was going to fail—because I couldn't control that. All I could do was fight for the city to the best of my ability. Putting all that pressure on myself wouldn't make me fight better—it would just distract me from doing my best.

From doing my duty.

I looked down, searching for the netting I'd dropped.

"There it is!" I whispered, spotting it in a crumpled heap on the roof of the building next to the armory. I plunged down and grabbed it, then draped it over my shoulder and darted across the armory roof to find Nathanael.

"Got it!" I cried as I sank down to float beside him. I peeked through the bars again, studying the collection of swords and spears and staffs and clubs we kept to protect the city from danger.

Surely Nathanael and I could defeat the serpent if we could just get to those weapons.

Nathanael chipped away at the sandstone between two of the bars. "The duels tournament is today," he said abruptly. "Wasn't it? Or it was supposed to be, anyway."

My chest ached. I drove my chisel into the sandstone, and a chunk of it crumbled.

"I suppose it's canceled," I said. "No one will remember to show up for it."

"We have bigger problems, anyway," he muttered.

What an understatement. Our mission was *way* more important than any competition. But it hurt to miss the tournament, all the same.

"I just wish none of this had happened," I said, scraping away at the crumbling stone.

The water clouded with sediment, obscuring my view of the window. I whirled around and flicked my fin at the cloudy water, wafting the worst of the sediment through the window.

"That's good!" Nathanael exclaimed, banging his chisel against the sandstone. "Could you keep doing that? It's hard to work with the water all murky."

I drove my chisel into the sandstone again, then spun around and swept away the cloudy water with a kick of my fin.

Nathanael tugged a bar out of the sandstone. "Got one!"

We fell into a steady rhythm until I felt dizzy from spinning back and forth—chisel at the sandstone, wave the murky water away, chisel at the sandstone, repeat. After a while, I gripped the edge of the window to steady myself.

"Ugh," I groaned. "I don't feel so good."

"We've got to keep going," said Nathanael as he broke the fourth bar free. "We're halfway there. Just a little long—"

A haunting melody drifted over the city. I froze, blinking rapidly, as if that would drive away the terrifying reality.

The seventh song unfolded all around us, coiling its terrifying tentacles around my heart.

The serpent was hunting for the last time.

The monster was about to feed.

Chapter Twenty-seven

Out of Time

Nathanael and I stared at each other.

My brother had frozen, his chisel still pressed against the sandstone. His hands trembled. The chisel slipped from his fingers and tipped over the edge of the window.

I dove forward, reaching through the open section of window and snatching the tool before it sank out of reach.

The song rolled on, the serpent's low, haunting voice constricting my chest.

Lightheadedness swept over me. My gills flared, and I thought my heart might leap out of my mouth.

It can't be. It's too soon.

"We're not ready!" Nathanael cried. "The serpent's about to eat the mer!"

I banged my hand against the next bar on the window, but it held fast in the sandstone.

"It doesn't matter if we're ready," I blurted, glancing down at the store of weapons. "We're out of time." My mind raced to come up with a solution, a new plan, anything. "Can you squeeze through the gap and grab the blades?"

My brother shook his head helplessly.

One look at the size of the opening told me it'd been a silly question. The window was only large enough to squeeze through if we took out *all* the bars.

The final notes of the song resounded, trilling over the city.

The seventh song fell silent.

Which meant the serpent was hunting on the reef, awaiting its final prey before it feasted.

Lyssa's face flashed in my mind. Then Lady Seraphina's. Then all the mer trapped in the serpent's lair, held fast in its strange netting.

Anger roared through me. There was only one thing left to do. *Fight for the city. Win or lose, live or die. Protect the people.*

"We have to go *now*," I exclaimed.

Nathanael's jaw dropped. "We're going to face off against the serpent with two chisels, two scrapers, and a net?" he demanded, throwing out his arms.

I offered him the chisel he'd dropped. "Do you have a better idea?" I asked in a small voice.

He threw back his head and groaned.

"I didn't think so," I said, straightening my back. "And we're fighting the serpent with more than just two chisels, two scrapers, and a net. We also have our fighting skills. Mother and Father sent us to train with Artemis so we could be prepared for a time like this."

"I doubt they thought we'd need combat training to take on a magical serpent before we even graduated school," he muttered, accepting the chisel.

"I'm sure they didn't imagine this exact situation." I managed a halfhearted chuckle. "But they knew that unforeseen threats would arise. And now one has."

I twisted the net together and tied it around my waist so it wouldn't slow me down as much, then pushed off the armory's sandstone and sliced through the water, soaring toward the reef.

Nathanael followed, grumbling.

For what felt like the thousandth time, I thought of my best friend, wrapped up in the serpent's cave.

I'll save you, Lyssa.

We reached the city wall, and I grabbed the edge of the stone with my free hand. My fingers traced the speckled, worn rock, its surface soft with algae.

"Look!" I pointed to the left.

A yellow-finned merman swam in a straight line over the reef, no doubt drawn by the serpent's song.

"Wait." Nathanael tapped his chisel on top of the wall. "That's not the direction of the lair. It's more that way. Remember? We passed that big rock coral!" He pointed at a rounded dome slightly to the right.

"But the serpent must be over there right now." I tilted my head toward the merman, who'd swum nearly out of sight, almost a speck in the water now.

"If we chase the serpent, though, we might not catch it in time. It might stay too many strokes ahead of us. Better to wait near its cave and attack it when it returns, right?"

I tilted my head, then nodded. "You're right. That's a great idea."

I tensed, preparing to launch forward.

Nathanael grabbed my arm. "Oh!" he hissed. I smacked at his hand, but he continued talking, unbothered. "I have an idea!"

I raised an eyebrow at him and picked a clump of algae off the wall to vent my boiling impatience.

"What if we don't *start* by attacking the serpent?" he asked.

My brow frumpled, and I stared at him. *What's he getting at?*

"Go on," I said slowly.

He clapped his hands, then poked me. "What if we stretch the netting over the cave entrance while the serpent is catching the next mer?"

"Brilliant! That'll buy us time, and keep it from getting into its lair and eating anyone!" I twitched my tail to knock my fin against his. "Together?"

He grabbed my hand. "Together."

"Let's go," we said in unison.

We shoved off the city wall and darted forward, swimming out over the reef.

The beautiful expanse of coral and fish opened up below us, and my thoughts drifted back to our class trip—the day I'd seen the serpent for the first time. Back when everything was simpler, and Lyssa was safe.

Lyssa will be safe, I told myself. *She has to be.*

I glanced down at my chisel and scraper. The tools had been forged for sharpness, to carve stone, but they weren't ideal weapons.

I spared a sideways glance at my brother, quill-pricks skittering down my spine. The makeshift bandage around his arm reminded me of his injury—of the injury *I'd* accidentally given him.

What if the bandage comes loose when we're fighting the serpent?

Would the smell of blood in the water draw the serpent to attack Nathanael? Or would we find ourselves fighting a shiver of frenzied sharks?

We swam through a school of yellow fish, then past a sting ray and a pair of turtles. I watched the bright coral, focusing on the patterns of the rocks, to help me remember where we were.

"Left here," I called, pointing at a familiar patch of coral. "The lair is this way."

Nathanael squinted, looking left and right, then nodded. We angled left, and I strained to see in the distance. Everything looked wrong.

Fear bobbed in my stomach like a floating jelly. What if we got lost and found the cave too late?

Then, in the distance, I glimpsed a rock formation. Hope rose in my throat.

There it is! A familiar opening in the rock. The tunnel.

"The serpent's lair," Nathanael whispered.

I thrashed my fin, propelling myself faster. We *had* to reach the cave before the serpent.

My mind fluttered to the duels tournament. To how badly I'd wanted to win, so Mother and Father and all the kids at school would realize I was capable.

I *still* wanted them to realize I was capable, but the competition seemed almost silly now.

At the end of this, would my parents be proud of us?

More than that, I hoped they'd realize I'd done my duty as crown princess—even if they locked me up in the palace for the rest of my life.

But ultimately, even if they didn't understand, I had to do this.

I had to do my duty, no matter what people thought about me. I'd give up everyone's good opinion if it meant my city was safe.

Because that's what queens do.

I tightened my grip on the tools as we swooped toward the tunnel.

I glanced from the hole to Nathanael, then unwrapped the netting from my shoulders and handed it to him. "Float here as a guard. Yell if you see the serpent coming."

"What are you going to do?" he asked with wide eyes.

I hefted my tools and stared at the lair. "I'm going to swim inside and make sure the serpent didn't beat us back."

I swam to the mouth of the cave and studied the rock face, finding three knob-like formations on its surface.

"When I give you the all-clear, stretch the netting over the tunnel by tying it to these knobs," I said, pointing at each protrusion.

He nodded seriously.

"Meanwhile, I'll use the tools to start cutting mer free," I continued.

"What happens when the serpent comes back?" he asked.

"When you see the serpent, yell out a warning, then swim away as fast as you can and find a hiding spot."

"But if it breaks through the net, you'll have to fight it all alone," he protested, crossing his arms.

"Do you have a better idea?" I lifted my chin in determination.

"I won't leave you to face danger by yourself, Sea Star," he insisted.

I grabbed his shoulder. "We don't have much time. Please, just go with this plan. You can keep me safe by warning me when the serpent returns. I won't be able to work if I'm worried about you putting yourself in danger."

He hesitated, his eyes awash in conflict.

Finally, he nodded. "Go, Sea Star. Free the mer."

Chapter Twenty-eight

THE SIGNAL

I squeezed Nathanael's shoulder and mouthed, "Thank you."

Then I flicked my fin and darted down the tunnel, my heart pounding. As I swam toward the lair, I blinked hard, willing my eyes to adjust to the dimness. I couldn't see yet, but I pushed forward at top speed anyway, ignoring the blind panic that threatened to close my throat.

This opens up into a large room. This opens up into a large room. This. Opens. Up. Into. A. Large. Room.

I sensed the tunnel walls fall away, sensed the serpent's lair open up around me. Again, I blinked, struggling to see if the serpent was here. My gills flared.

All lay still. Then I heard a bubbling snore to my right. The cocooned mer slumbered around me, lulled into deep relaxation by the serpent's song.

Finally, I could make out the shapes in the circular room. I looked this way and that, slumping in relief. The serpent hadn't returned. I was alone with the captured mer.

"Cover the entrance!" I yelled down the tunnel.

First things first. Free the mer.

I swam across the room to Lyssa. "Hey," I murmured when I reached her cocoon. "Lyssa, wake up. I'm here to save you."

Carefully, I used the chisel to pull a chunk of the serpent's strange netting—*webbing*, Lady Seraphina's tablet had called it—away from Lyssa's body, then sliced through it with the scraper.

Lyssa groaned and mumbled something indecipherable.

"Wake up, sleepyhead," I replied. "I'm getting you out of here."

"El?" Lyssa asked through a yawn.

Relief flooded my stomach at the sound of her voice. I sliced through another chunk of netting.

"I'm here, Lyssa," I said. Two more slices, and I'd opened Lyssa's cocoon. I gently eased her out of the webbing and pointed across the room at the tunnel.

"I know you're tired and everything seems fine," I said, hoping the urgency in my voice would cut through the siren enchantment. "But I need you to swim over there and wait below that hole. If anything happens—if that monster comes inside—swim through the hole and go back to the city, okay?"

"Mmmkayyyyyy," she muttered, rubbing her eyes.

At least she had a chance of escaping, if . . . if my fight with the serpent went badly.

I gave her a gentle shove, then moved to the next cocoon, freeing the merman inside and giving him the same instructions I'd given Lyssa. He sleepily agreed and drifted toward Lyssa, who was curled up in a ball on the seafloor directly underneath the tunnel.

I reached the next cocoon, which was smaller than the others.

A child? I sliced through the webbing. When I reached for the mer inside, my fingers touched something hard and rubbery, entirely unlike mer skin.

I squinted at the shadowy outline. My jaw dropped when I realized I was looking at a young dolphin.

"Hey," I whispered. "Easy there." I coaxed the dolphin out of the cocoon and murmured, "Guess I can't explain the plan to you." I gently shoved the dolphin toward Lyssa and the merman, hoping it would follow them to safety when the time came.

I darted to the next cocoon. Just as I cut through the first chunk of netting, I heard a distant yell.

"Sea Star!" Nathanael cried from outside.

I swallowed hard. *The signal.*

The serpent had returned from its hunt.

I sliced through another chunk of webbing. I'd only freed two mer. I could only hope the netting at the mouth of the cave did its job and kept the serpent out until I could finish freeing the others.

My hands trembled as I sliced through the final chunk of netting and guided a yawning mermaid out of her cocoon.

"Float over there, and wait with those two mer, okay?" I smiled when I saw the young dolphin resting on the seafloor at Lyssa's side. "If the monster comes inside, swim through the tunnel and get to the city as fast as you can."

"Sssssure," the mermaid said slowly.

I pushed her toward Lyssa just as a low-pitched howl chilled my blood. The cave shook. I darted to the next cocoon and sliced through the webbing.

The serpent was trying to break into the cave.

I worked as quickly as I could, sending one more mermaid to wait with Lyssa.

I'd just reached the sixth cocoon when the howl sounded again. I cut open a chunk of netting, and the howl grew unmistakably louder.

I whirled around, my gills flaring. There wasn't time to free the others.

The serpent crashed through the tunnel and into the lair, our net hanging off its head like a veil. Its beady eyes scanned the room, then locked on me.

It coiled in a circle, ready to strike.

Chapter Twenty-Nine
Onto the Reef

I held perfectly still, my gaze locked on the monster. Cold chills tingled through my blood.

This is it. I'm going to die.

I hadn't realized until now how big the monster was. Its keen, intelligent eyes studied me, as if searching my soul.

"Get out of here!" I screamed. "Go!"

Though I was staring at the serpent, I intended my words for Lyssa and the other freed mer.

Please hear me. Please get out of here.

In my periphery, I saw Lyssa twitch, then glance up at the serpent's long, thin belly.

"Go!" I yelled again.

Lyssa grabbed the dolphin's dorsal fin, and the two of them swam toward the tunnel.

After a brief pause, the two mermaids and the merman followed at a nonchalant pace.

I waved my arms at the serpent to keep its attention—so it wouldn't realize that half its prey was escaping. Then I caught sight of the yellow-tailed merman held in the serpent's coiled tail.

"If you want to eat any of my people," I yelled, brandishing the chisel. "You're gonna have to eat me first!"

The serpent stared at me. Then opened its mouth. And began to sing.

The melody rippled over me, low and beautiful. I couldn't help but feel certain the serpent was singing straight to me.

It thought it could lull me into the same relaxation that had befallen the rest of the city.

But it couldn't.

I am the daughter of Queen Hanna and King Demetrios—a descendant of sirens on one side and the Crown Princess of Thessalonike on the other. And you will not take my people.

The song rang on. I tightened my grip on my makeshift weapons, preparing to strike at the serpent, scanning its body, searching for weak points.

Scales, like a webbed-foot dragon, I noted. That would make the fight harder.

Could my chisel pierce its scales?

If only we'd been able to get the weapons from the armory!

I assumed a fighting stance, watching for the monster to flinch, waiting for it to make the first move.

Every moment of delay gave Lyssa and the others more time to make it back to the city.

The serpent uncurled its tail, releasing the merman caught in its grasp. The merman stretched out and gave a cavernous yawn, then sank to the seafloor, asleep.

"Get out of here!" I yelled at him.

But he didn't hear me.

I snapped my attention back to the serpent. Its tail slowly coiled forward. I hovered just above the seafloor, ready to—

Thwack!

The tail snapped toward me. I dove forward, darting underneath it.

It smacked against the stone wall—right above an empty cocoon.

I whirled around, registering the dent the tail had left in the stone, and swallowed the bile that scalded my throat.

Now I floated directly beneath the serpent. I propelled myself upward, charging as fast as I could at its underbelly.

If this monster was anything like webbed-foot dragons, the underbelly would be easier to pierce.

Thwack!

Pain lanced through me as the serpent's mighty tail collided with my fin.

I whirled through the water, struggling to right myself, struggling to figure out which way was up, where the serpent was.

I hit the wall and grunted. Nausea washed over me. Everything in me wanted to sink to the seafloor to regain my bearings, but I didn't have time.

The tail swung at me again, and I ducked away from it.

Thwack!

It smacked the cave wall, just a hand's width above my head.

This isn't working.

I urged my heart to slow, reminded myself to stay calm.

What would Artemis tell me to do?

As I locked eyes with the serpent again, the memory unfurled in my mind. *Always pace yourself, and you'll make fewer tactical mistakes.*

I was already starting to tire, and my head hurt from the collision with the wall. I needed to pace myself.

Another of Artemis's lessons: *Fight smarter. Keep your wits about you.*

This monster was faster than me, and stronger. But I was smarter.

I glanced at the empty, dangling cocoons, then at the stone wall behind them. The serpent's tail was strong enough to crack the stone.

How to fight smarter?

Facing off against the serpent inside this cave was a terrible idea. It played to the serpent's strengths rather than mine, and made encounters with that whip of a tail even more dangerous.

But I couldn't escape down the tunnel—the serpent would catch me before I made it halfway to the reef.

I glanced again at the cracked stone, and an idea streamed into my mind.

Its tail flashed forward again, and I darted upward.

Crash!

It struck the rock wall *beneath* me.

My heart pounded. It had hit the wall just *lower* than where I'd been floating a moment ago. My mind raced over that piece of information.

The serpent had seen me feint downward twice and anticipated I'd do it again. It was learning my tactics.

Maybe it's smarter than I gave it credit for.

The thought chilled my blood.

I glanced at the cave ceiling.

How thick is that stone? I tried to mentally compare the height of this cavern with the height of the rock face I'd seen on the reef.

What if . . .

"Come and get me!" I taunted, floating higher.

If I tricked the serpent into smashing the cave ceiling with its tail, maybe it would break through the stone, forming an opening that would let me move the battle onto the reef.

But this time, the serpent dove straight at me.

I plunged toward the seafloor, barely avoiding its snapping jaws. Something jerked my tail, and I whirled around with a shriek, swinging wildly through the water.

Webbing!

A string of webbing encircled my tail, just above my fin, tying me to the serpent.

I was caught!

The serpent flipped around, beady eyes on me. The webbing tugged at my fin. The serpent glided forward, surrounding me.

It's wrapping me in one of its cocoons!

I curled forward and stretched out my arm, scraper extended. *I don't think so, you scrawny dragon . . .*

With a final push, I sliced through the string, then dove through a gap between the looping coils of the serpent's body. With a tight grip on the chisel, I drove the sharp point against the dull blue-and-green scales.

The chisel bounced off the serpent, the ricochet shooting pain up my arm.

The serpent let out that low, bone-chilling howl.

I swam toward the ceiling again, cold fear gripping me.

Fight smarter, I heard Artemis's voice in my head. *If something happens to your weapon, you have to find whatever you can and use it to fight.*

I still had the chisel, but it hadn't pierced the serpent's armor.

I glanced wildly around the cave.

What could I use as a weapon? What might work better than the carving tools?

And, more importantly, how could I get the serpent out onto the reef?

Then I heard a voice I knew and loved so well.

"Hey, you silly-shaped serpent!" Nathanael called in a singsong from somewhere in the tunnel. "Don't I sound delicious to eat?"

The serpent snapped to attention, narrowing its pupils, craning its neck to peer down the tunnel.

"No, Nathanael!" I yelled. "Hide!"

But my brother wasn't deterred. "Nah-nah-nah-nah!" he sang. "Hey! I think I'm a better singer than you are!"

The serpent charged for the tunnel, its long, thin body uncoiling into a straight line.

"Swim!" I screamed. "It's coming fast!"

The serpent reached the tunnel. Its head, then body, then tail disappeared into the hole, like the tunnel was swallowing it up.

I looked at the remaining cocoons hanging from the walls, then at the tunnel.

"I'm sorry!" I called to the trapped mer. Then I flicked my fin and swam for the tunnel.

Nathanael couldn't fight that thing on his own. He didn't know what it was capable of. And while we were fighting the serpent on the reef, these mer wouldn't be any safer out in the open than in this cave.

I plunged into the hole in the rock, extending my arms and hurtling toward my brother and the monster.

A window of light shone ahead of me, oppressively bright after the darkness of the cave. I blinked hard.

All at once, I burst out onto the reef, the light streaming from the surface sending searing pain shooting through my eyes.

Whirling, I blinked again, trying to acclimate, searching for my brother.

Then I spotted them. Nathanael and the monster, hovering, staring at each other.

The monster seemed... different, somehow. Its stance didn't seem nearly as aggressive. Its blue-and-green scales gleamed in the light, and the pink fans along its spine lay flat.

"Sea Star?" Nathanael called, his voice trembling. "What's it doing?"

I darted toward my brother, sweeping between him and the monster.

But the serpent didn't look at me. It gazed past me, studying Nathanael. Another of Artemis's lessons echoed in my mind: *Pay attention to the eyes.*

In the serpent's eyes, I saw... curiosity. Openness. Nothing like the venomous hunger I'd seen in the cave.

"M-maybe it... likes you?" I stuttered.

Nathanael swam forward, stopping when he floated side-by-side with me.

"The chisels don't pierce its scales!" I exclaimed. "We'll need to improvise and figure out some new weapons."

He clicked his tongue. "Um... what can we find out here?"

My mind raced, sorting through different kinds of coral Calandra had taught me about. "Maybe something poisonous would work?"

"But how would we get the poison into its blood?" Nathanael asked. "We need to pierce its scales."

The serpent squinted at us, its open curiosity shifting to something hungrier. The pink fans on its back stood straight up.

Then its body coiled.

Chapter Thirty
SERPENT EYES

"Uh-oh!" I said, staring at the coiling serpent hovering above the reef.

"What's it doing now?" Nathanael whispered.

I backed away. "It's going to strike at us with its tail. Move away slowly."

An octopus floated past us on a current, eyes closed, tentacles trailing, looking entirely un-octopuslike.

Bewitched, I thought grimly. *Cursed siren magic.*

I shoved Nathanael behind me and gripped my chisel.

"Its scales aren't vulnerable," I said. "But it's got to have a weakness."

"Maybe its eyes?" he offered.

My gaze flicked to the serpent's eyes. They glinted, reflecting the light in shades of gold and green. A shudder flashed through me. For some reason, they made me uncomfortable.

Pay attention to the eyes.

"When it lunges," I whispered, "you swim right and I'll swim left. Then we'll—"

The tail flashed forward, and I jerked left, unable to finish my sentence. I thrashed my fin, swimming fast. Then the serpent dove at me, teeth bared.

I plunged toward the seafloor, hurtled around a large rock, and darted through a purple coral archway.

The serpent followed.

"Sea Star!" Nathanael screamed. "Swim!"

But I didn't need the warning. The serpent snapped at me. Hot pain shot through my body as its teeth closed on the very edge of my fin, tugging me off course. I spiraled helplessly in a wide circle, then tore myself free, the momentum carrying me forward.

I bit down on my tongue to suppress a scream and crashed onto the rounded top of a rock coral.

My tail burned. My head pounded. My whole body felt battered and bruised. I sensed the serpent hovering over me, casting an icy shadow. I tensed, waiting for its jaws to clamp down.

"Hey, you smelly serpent!" Nathanael yelled. "Bet you can't catch me!"

With a groan, I flipped over. Blood curled up from the wound on my tail in ethereal threads. My hand flew to my mouth. *Blood in the water. On the reef.*

And then those fears disappeared as my brother darted at the serpent. Chisel extended, he soared toward the monster's head, aiming for the eyes.

"Don't!" I yelled.

The monster's tail flashed around. As if in slow motion, the tail wrapped around Nathanael's waist one, two, three times. It swung around, wrenching Nathanael away. My brother yelled.

Then the serpent looped around him, wrapping him in sticky black threads.

I forgot all about the pain—in my tail, in my head, everywhere—and jolted upward.

"Sea Star!" Nathanael called. "Help!"

The serpent encircled him, but through the gaps in its looping body I could just barely make out what was happening. The monster had wrapped up Nathanael's fin and half his tail already.

My gills flared, my pulse pounding in my ears. For several heartbeats, everything fell away. The ocean was utterly silent. There was only me, the monster, and my brother.

And I wouldn't let anything happen to Nathanael. No matter what.

The fear fell away, and I stiffened my back.

Fight smarter, Artemis would say. *Study your enemy.*

What had worked against the serpent? We couldn't get the upper hand fighting it, but . . . *Nathanael managed to distract it.*

"Nah-nah-nah-nah!" I sang, echoing my brother's lilting taunt that had caught the serpent's attention earlier. "Hey! I think I'm a better singer—"

The serpent's head snapped toward me, and it froze. For an unending moment, I held its gaze. Those gold-and-green eyes studied me, squinting, no longer aggressive and hungry but . . . curious and almost gentle.

It worked! I almost couldn't believe it.

Its body uncoiled, and it swam toward me slowly. Nathanael wriggled out of its loosening grip, then sank to the seafloor, unable to propel himself through the water with his fin bound up. I watched him with my peripheral vision but kept my gaze fixed on the serpent.

"Nah-nah-nah-nah!" I sang again.

The serpent's eyes widened, and it lowered its neck as it floated toward me.

"Careful!" Nathanael yelled.

But, somehow, I knew the serpent wasn't coming in for an attack. Not this time.

Quillpricks tingled on my skin. What was happening? Why did that schoolreef taunt calm the monster?

And then it hit me.

Siren song.

Nathanael and I resisted the serpent's enchantments because of our siren blood. Siren magic flowed in our veins, however weakly.

And when we sang, we calmed the serpent, somehow. Because it recognized our magic.

In a soprano voice, I sang, "Don't hurt us, please."

"What are you doing?" Nathanael called. With the chisel, he tore at the webbing around his fin.

I answered in song, "It likes it when we sing."

"Ohhhhhh," he said, lilting his voice up at the end, making the word more songlike.

At that faint trace of music, the serpent swiveled to look at Nathanael.

"What do we do now?" Nathanael sang to me.

Pain throbbed through me again, and I pressed my hand against my tail wound to try to staunch the thin line of blood.

"We have to get out of here," I lilted. "There's blood in the water."

The serpent glanced back at me, seeming almost confused. If it'd had eyebrows, I think it would have furrowed them. Then it looked back at the cave, and a rumble growled from its stomach.

It swam past me at a dignified pace, gliding toward the cave.

Nathanael and I stared at each other.

"No!" I exclaimed.

I swam after the serpent, pain searing each time I kicked my fin. Nathanael, uninjured, caught up with me just as I reached the serpent. I floated in front of the creature and crossed my arms.

"Please don't eat the mer!" I sang.

The serpent's stomach rumbled again.

"It's not enough, Sea Star." Nathanael poked my arm, and I winced. It felt like I had bruises all over.

The serpent angled left and swam around us.

We hurried after it, and Nathanael said, "It's not going to attack *us* anymore, but it still wants to eat the mer!"

"El!" a familiar voice called lazily across the reef. "What are you doing out here?"

I whirled, looking toward the city. Lyssa swam toward us, her magenta hair streaming behind her. My stomach sank to the seafloor.

"Go home!" I yelled, waving my arms. "Go back to the city!"

From the corner of my eye, I saw the serpent stop. Then turn.

My hands trembled. *No, no, no, no!*

The serpent fixed its eyes on Lyssa and coiled to strike.

Chapter Thirty-one

THE DUETS TOURNAMENT

"Let her leave!" I sang, trying to catch the serpent's attention.

It spared a glance at me. Then its stomach rumbled again, and it stared hungrily at Lyssa.

I darted forward, floating between my friend and the creature.

"Look at me!" I sang. "Ignore her."

Again, its eyes flicked to me, but only for a moment. Then it floated menacingly forward, fixated on Lyssa.

Nathanael followed, hovering at my side, his arms crossed. "Didn't the sirens tame this thing?" he asked. "With the magic they stole from Shiloh?"

"What about it?" I couldn't remember.

I couldn't focus on that snippet of memory with Lyssa in danger.

Evening light hit the water, softening the ocean's shining surface to a lustrous rose gold and filtering down over the reef in warm tones.

"The caecelias—those octopus-mer people—had a famous show," Nathanael said.

"Right. I remember that part. They enchanted the fish to talk like caecelias."

The serpent glided forward, casting a shadow over us.

"Stay back!" I yelled at it. We paddled backward to keep ourselves between the monster and Lyssa.

My brother continued, "But they didn't *just* give the fish caecelia voices! They couldn't have. It wouldn't make any sense!"

I furrowed my brow. "Why not?" I asked, swimming backward, though the truth was slowly beginning to dawn on me too.

"What would a fish say if it could talk?" Nathanael asked.

My gaze drifted to a clownie floating lazily next to her magenta anemone. After a long pause, I offered, "Blub?"

"Exactly!" exclaimed Nathanael. "Fish aren't smart. They're not anything like mer or caecelias or sirens—or even like dolphins."

"So, for a fish to speak with the voice of a caecelia," I said slowly, "the magic would have to . . . make the fish smarter? No, that's not quite right, is it?"

Nathanael shook his head. "The magic would have to—"

"Connect the fish's mind to the caecelia's!" I shouted.

"Yes!" Nathanael exclaimed. Then he tilted his head and stared up at the serpent. "But why can't we communicate with it, then? It's like it recognizes us . . . recognizes the magic in our song, but it can't understand us."

"Like we don't have enough magic," I said. Then I jolted upward, understanding flowing through me.

"Sea Star?" Nathanael asked, puzzled, looking at me.

"We don't have enough magic," I exclaimed, "because we don't have much siren blood. Like how we can't fully enchant people, but we still don't sing in public because mer will be too drawn to us."

"Like how Father fell in love with Mother!" Nathanael hit the side of his head.

"Exactly!" My back collided with something solid, and I pivoted to find Lyssa there.

I snapped my attention back to the serpent. It coiled its scaly body, preparing a strike.

"Lyssa, get down!" I screamed, whirling around and shoving her toward the seafloor. As the serpent's tail flashed forward, I threw my body over Lyssa's and squeezed my eyes tight, bracing for the impact.

But nothing came.

I peeked at the monster. Its neck curved forward, and its head floated down to meet me. It still didn't want to hurt me.

"You can't eat her," I sang, clinging to Lyssa's shoulders, trying to make the serpent understand.

Underneath me, Lyssa mumbled, "What's going on, El?"

"Stay still," I hissed. "Don't catch its attention."

The serpent held my gaze. I didn't look away. I sat up straight and crossed my arms. "You can't eat mer," I sang.

Nathanael darted to my side and mimicked my pose. With my brother next to me, I dared a glance down at my fin. The bleeding had stopped, a scab forming on the wound, but it still throbbed with pain.

Nathanael, the serpent, and I stayed there, locked in a standoff, for a few long moments. Then I glanced at Nathanael and almost gasped aloud. With his fierce, protective face and unmovable stance, he looked so much older.

And he looked so much like Mother.

Mother...

Would *she* be able to communicate with the serpent? Did she have enough siren blood?

Discomfort twinged in my chest. Whether she could communicate with it or not, it was far too late to go back to the city and find her—the serpent would eat the mer in the lair before we returned.

My fingertips tingled. We were going to have to fight the serpent again. And I wasn't sure we could win.

"Nathanael, we—" I glanced at my brother again. He still looked so much like Mother.

All at once, the truth flooded me. *Mother told us that even full-blooded sirens sing together, with many voices, while bewitching a city.*

Hope awakened in my chest.

"What?" Nathanael asked.

I grabbed his hand. "We have just enough siren magic for the serpent to recognize us—but not enough for it to understand us."

"Right," he said like it was obvious. "We figured that out already."

Squeezing his hand, I said, "Sing a duet with me. Sing Mother's lullaby."

His mouth opened in surprise, and I plunged ahead, singing, "Sleep, little love. The surface fades from gold to black."

He joined me on the next line, harmonizing. "Sleep, little love. Rest safely, nothing lack."

I locked eyes again with the serpent, and we sang on, growing more confident with each line. "Sleep, little love. May currents gently rock your bed. Sleep, little love, lay down your weary head."

The serpent blinked, and something flashed through those intelligent eyes. I felt sure it understood our song.

My soprano trilled out over the reef, Nathanael still singing the harmony. "Sleep, little love, tomorrow will be time for jest. Sleep, little love. The fishes bid you rest."

The serpent's blinks grew slower. It uncoiled and sank to the seafloor. First its tail bumped the rock coral, and then the rest of its long, winding body came to rest atop the reef. It gave a great, gaping yawn.

"A duets tournament instead of a duels tournament," Nathanael said.

I shoved him with my shoulder. "Same tune, but we're going to tell it that it can't eat mer." Then I remembered the little dolphin I'd freed from the cave. "Or dolphins!" I added.

Quickly, we worked out alternate lyrics and turned back to the serpent. "Don't hunt the mer. The reef has lots of fish to eat."

The serpent tilted its head.

We continued singing, "Don't eat the mer. And spare the dolphins too."

The serpent's tongue flicked in and out of its mouth, and it lay its head down, looking deeply dejected.

Unexpected sympathy flashed through me.

It's so hungry. I wished I could bring it food—enough fish for a feast.

I rattled off another set of lyrics to Nathanael, and we sang, "Don't eat the mer. We're here to free them from the cave."

This lullaby didn't rhyme, but it didn't matter—the serpent's body language said it understood. It let out a mournful howl.

"That howl must be its natural sound," I murmured to Nathanael. "From before the sirens enchanted it."

Lyssa squirmed out from beneath me and scrambled to face the now-docile serpent, her magenta hair floating around her face. "El?" Her voice trembled.

"You're awake!" I exclaimed, pulling her into a hug.

She held me tight. "Everything is so fuzzy," she said. "The memories are fuzzy. But I . . . I think I followed the song out onto the reef. Then I was in a dark place for a long time, but I was happy." She pulled back and looked down at her arms. "Fishes and wishes! Did I die? Are we dead? What was that place?"

"A cocoon. You're alive. I'll explain everything later," I replied.

She spun back around, watching the serpent. "It's all like a dream. In my dream, you pulled me out of that dark place and gave me a"—her forehead wrinkled—"a dolphin?"

I just smiled and gestured for her to continue.

"Then I was almost at the city and decided to come back. I don't know why. Out on the reef, I saw you and . . . somehow ended up here with you? Then you and Nathanael started singing, and I think I fell asleep."

"Well, we did sing a lullaby," Nathanael said.

Lyssa pointed at the serpent. "What is it doing?" she asked tremulously. "I woke up, and you were singing again, about it not eating us, and it was like the song lyrics cut through all the . . . murkiness in my head and I realized . . . what have I been doing? I should be terrified of that thing and—"

"I'll explain everything," I assured her. "But I don't think it's going to hurt anyone. Not anymore."

A sob choked her. "Thank you for saving me. I love you two so much."

Movement flashed out of the corner of my eye. As one, we spun. I tried to make sense of the large, imposing shape hurtling toward me.

Lyssa let out a scream.

A shark.

Chapter Thirty-two

Shark Attack

Not just any shark.

A great shark—the most fearsome shark in the ocean.

And it was swimming straight at me.

My fin! Blood in the water. I'd stopped bleeding, but not before the blood had attracted sharks. My mind stuttered. I'd gotten myself injured on the reef and drawn a shark here—so near the city.

"Swim!" I yelled.

We darted away, but as I whirled around, I glimpsed two more sharks advancing on us from the other side. Distracted, I slammed into a pillar coral. Pain shot through me as my fin wound tore open again.

Oh no.

A thin line of blood seeped through my scales and rose into the darkening water.

Nathanael grabbed my hand and tugged me upward.

Then the sharks vanished in a blur of blue-and-green scales and pink fins. The serpent's body coiled around us—not tightly, like it was trying to wrap us up. It curled loosely, surrounding us like the walls of a cave. Like it was ... shielding us from the sharks. A shadow loomed over us, and I looked up to find the serpent peering down, hungry question in its eager eyes.

Nathanael poked my arm and shouted, "Same tune! Tell it, 'Please eat the sharks. In fact we would appreciate it!'"

We burst into song. Our impromptu lyric had one too many syllables for the line of music, and our voices hit screechingly jarring notes at the end. Lyssa covered her ears, grimacing, but the bad music didn't seem to bother the serpent.

Its tongue flicked in and out, and then the end of its tail snaked toward us.

"What—" Nathanael asked as the tail looped around the three of us.

Lyssa screamed, and panic gripped my chest.

Had I misread the serpent's body language? Had it been luring us into a trap so we'd let down our guard?

Then, all of a sudden, we swept through the water so fast my stomach dropped out from under me. I glimpsed four . . . no, five . . . no, six sharks!

The serpent's tail loosened its grip. I spun free of Lyssa and Nathanael and collided with a wall of rock. I blinked, pressing my back against the rock to try to regain my bearings.

Nathanael and Lyssa hovered in front of me, and the serpent . . .

The serpent was charging back at the shiver of sharks. It reached the first one and encircled it, spinning so fast it looked like a blur. Then I heard that melody again—that haunting song floating out to us on the current. The serpent was singing to lull the sharks.

Lyssa visibly relaxed, falling under the enchantment. Nathanael and I winced and stared at each other.

"We're going to have to tell the serpent that it can't sing this close to the city," he muttered.

"Agreed," I said. "But I think that can wait until it's taken care of these sharks."

The great sharks stopped ominously circling, instead floating lazily, as if they'd forgotten about the blood. The serpent finished wrapping up the first great shark and dropped it, letting it sink to the reef, encased in the silvery-black webbing. With a graceful flip, the serpent dove toward another shark.

Glancing from Nathanael to Lyssa, I said, "Let's sing to wake Lyssa up."

We hastily put together the lyrics and sang, "Wake up, Lyssa. Remember where you are."

Lyssa startled back to alertness, rubbing her head with a groan.

"Thanks again. You're the best," she said, her voice emotional. "My head still feels soooooo fuzzy. Remind me never to chase a monster onto the reef again."

Then I realized we were floating right next to the serpent's tunnel.

"The lair!" I exclaimed, pointing at the hole in the rock just above us. "Let's go! The sharks are too big to fit through there."

Nathanael eyed the scene skeptically. "I don't think they're going to follow us, anyway."

The serpent finished wrapping up the second shark, then glided effortlessly toward a great shark entranced by a green anemone.

I chewed on my lip. "I think you're right," I said. "But let's go free the mer. I don't think the serpent is going to try to stop us anymore."

"Looks like it has plenty to eat," added Lyssa, rolling her shoulders like she was trying to get rid of a chill.

Nathanael waved his chisel. "I lost the scraper, but I still have this."

I chuckled and held up my empty hands. "My tools are long since lost, but I think if we all work together, we'll get everyone out of there in no time. Are there any sharp rocks we could use?"

"There were some rocks in the lair." Lyssa rubbed her eyes. "After you freed me, I . . . did I lie down at the bottom of the cave?"

"Yep," I replied. "I told you to wait on the cavern floor, near the tunnel, in case the serpent came back."

Lyssa nodded slowly, blinking hard. "There were some small rocks there—about the size of my hand. At least one of them was kind of sharp. It annoyed me, but for some reason, I didn't think to move it."

"The serpent's enchantment," I said. "It muddled your brain."

"Let's go!" called Nathanael. He darted down the tunnel, Lyssa following him.

I paused for a long moment, watching the serpent, then—carefully, trying to swim more with my arms than with my injured fin—followed them.

We emerged into the lair, and I blinked, willing my eyes to adjust to the dimness.

The yellow-finned merman slumbered on the rocky seafloor, curled into a ball. We swam down to the seafloor, and Lyssa and I each picked out a sharp stone. As the dark cave came into focus, I counted the bundles.

Five hung off the cave wall in tatters, but there were still four more mer entrapped.

"Come on!" I said.

We swam to the nearest bundle and pulled at the sticky webbing, awkwardly cutting through it with our rocks and the chisel.

When we'd opened the cocoon, I recognized the merman inside—this was the soldier from our day on the reef, the one who'd acted so carelessly about the blood in the water. Gently, we guided him down to wait with the yellow-finned merman, and he curled up and fell back asleep. One by one, we freed the others—last of all, Lady Seraphina.

When we'd brought Lady Seraphina down to the group of slumbering mer, I said, "Let's sing them awake."

To the tune of Mother's lullaby, my brother and I sang, "Wake, merfolk, wake. We must return to home."

The five mer lifted their heads, blinking and yawning. I met Lady Seraphina's eyes, and she murmured, "Princess Eliana? What's happened?"

"I'll explain everything," I assured her. "For now, let's get back to the city."

"Follow me!" cried Nathanael. He led the way to the tunnel, and Lyssa and I took up the rear, ensuring that not a single mer was left behind.

My heart beat a little faster as we swam through the tunnel. Had the serpent taken care of all the sharks? Would we face any danger on the reef?

But my fears evaporated when Lyssa and I broke into the dusky light. Five large cocoons lay motionless on the reef. The serpent twisted toward us, a shark's tail fin dangling from its mouth. The serpent took a great gulp and swallowed the rest of the shark whole.

I swam toward it—swam toward *him*, for I realized I'd recognized it was a boy serpent when we started singing to him—and he curled his long neck down until his head hovered in front of me.

I rested a hand on his nose, and my brother joined me. Lyssa swam on, guiding the rescued mer toward the city.

"Let's tell him that we'll be back to see him soon, if we can," I said. "And . . . let's say *thank you*—for not eating the mer, and for his help with the sharks."

Nathanael poked my arm. "Plus, we need to tell him to not sing anywhere near the city. And . . . we could ask if he'd keep patrolling the reef? He can hunt any fish he wants, but he can especially stay on the lookout for sharks and webbed-foot dragons."

I brightened at the idea. "He can help keep the city safe!"

We worked out the lyrics, and then we began to sing.

Chapter Thirty-three

CONFESSIONS

Nathanael and I floated just outside Mother and Father's bedchamber. The familiar palace corridor felt normal and comforting after a very, very long day.

"Ready?" my brother asked with a grimace.

I clenched my hands into fists. "Ready," I replied, suppressing a yawn.

Night had fallen over the city, but it was time to wake the king from the siren enchantment.

Sure, Father would wake from the enchantment on his own in the next day or two—but it was time for Nathanael and me to let go of some of the responsibility we'd been carrying.

Someday, like Father, I'd have to worry about the city's safety all the time. But this experience had been more than enough of a trial swim for now. I'd be relieved when things went back to normal.

Well, *relatively normal*.

Once Nathanael and I explained everything to Mother and Father, we'd probably be locked in the palace for a whole year. Or the rest of our lives. But I hoped they'd let us visit the serpent from time to time. I already felt a bond to him.

What a difference from a few hours ago!

I tapped on the doorframe.

"Who is it?" called Mother, distress in her voice.

"It's us!" I shifted uncomfortably.

A long pause lingered in the water, then Mother bolted through the privacy curtain, a volcanic scowl on her face.

"Where have you children been?" she demanded. "I searched for you everywhere! I tried to call out the Royal Mer Guard to scour the city to find you, but they were too enchanted to hold the thought in their heads long enough to conduct a search! Why did you disappear? Where did you go? What—"

I raised my hand halfway. "Can . . . we come in? We need to explain this to Father, too, and I'd rather only have to admit to everything once."

Her eyes narrowed in suspicion. "Admit to . . . everything? What did you two do?" Then she threw out her hands. "Your father won't remember anything if you tell him right now. He's still bewitched."

Nathanael and I glanced at each other, and I gave Mother a nervous smile. "Well . . . we can fix that," I said.

Mother stared at us. "You can fix what?"

"We can un-enchant Father."

Her brow furrowed in confusion.

"Just let us come in?" squeaked Nathanael.

She floated to the side and let us swim past her. Father rolled over, mumbling. Feeling small, I sank into the oversized hammock chair across the room, Nathanael at my side.

We glanced at each other and launched into the song we'd practiced on the way home. "Wake, Father, wake. The city's been enchaaa-anted." We threw in an extra syllable on *enchanted* to fit the line of music.

Father rolled over again, then sat bolt upright in the hammock.

Nathanael and I sang the next line. "Wake, Father, wake. We have so much to tell you now."

Father's bushy eyebrows drew together, and he stared at us. "What is it? What's happened, children?" He rubbed his temples. "What's happened to me?"

Mother swept to his side and wrapped her arms around him. "Demetrios!" she cried. "You're back!" Then her attention snapped back to us. "You children have a lot of explaining to do." Though her voice was stern, her face had softened.

I plunged ahead. "So, remember that monster I saw on the reef?"

To Mother and Father's credit, they let us tell the story with very few interruptions—although when I said that the serpent bit my fin, Father leaped up from the hammock, muttering that he'd kill it with his bare hands.

"Stop!" Nathanael cried. "We're not done!"

When we finally finished, we folded our hands and waited in silence. Dread coiled in my stomach like the serpent's tail before a strike. How mad would they be? I wasn't used to getting in trouble. I didn't like to pull pranks like Nathanael did.

Father looked pale, and his gills flared. "I almost can't believe it," he murmured.

I nodded quickly. I knew the story sounded crazy. "We brought back the mer we rescued," I said. "Lady Seraphina is waiting in the throne room in case you want to ask her any questions."

"What were you thinking?" Mother finally snapped. "You children went out on the reef alone to fight a monster? What would have happened if it had eaten you?"

But Father rested a hand on her shoulder. "Hanna," he said softly. "They saved the city." Pride shone in his eyes. "They remembered the lesson we've instilled in them since they were small."

"Protect the people," I whispered.

He swam forward and knelt in front of us, taking my hands in his. "Yes, Eliana. Above all else, we protect the people."

My dread evaporated, replaced by hope. "So, you're not mad?" I asked.

"I'm mad!" exclaimed Mother, but she didn't sound entirely convinced

Father turned to Nathanael and rested a hand on his head. "You children will be incredible guardians for the city someday." He chuckled in a half-bewildered way. "I suppose you already are."

I basked in the praise, feeling warm all over.

"But," he added, his usual sternness overtaking him, "the two of you are *not* to go swimming off to fight danger like that unless you have exhausted *every* alternative." He held both of his hands up. "This hero business will *not* become a regular occurrence. Am I quite understood?"

"Yes, Father," Nathanael and I said in unison.

"Now," said Father, looking back at me. "Let's go wake one of the healers and let them take care of your fin, Eliana. We don't want it to get infected."

I bit down on a knuckle. "Father?"

His gentle eyes met mine. "Yes, my dear?"

"Nathanael and I will have to go out to the reef and visit the serpent sometimes. It's bonded to siren song, and we can talk to it. If we spend time with it, I think it'll help safeguard the city from great sharks and webbed-foot dragons."

Father's lips twitched, and he glanced at Mother. "Your mother and I will need to have a long talk about what all this magic means, I think. I don't understand it well enough to say yes or no."

But this time, it was Mother who shakily smiled. "I saw this magic many times in Shiloh, Demetrios. The caecelias could enchant any creature—even dangerous ones. I think Eliana is right—we are far safer with the serpent in service to the city, guided by Eliana and Nathanael, than we would be if we drove it off."

At that, Father looked thoughtful.

"One more thing, Father?" I blurted.

He chuckled. "Yes, Eliana?"

"The duels tournament was supposed to be today," I said. "But obviously it didn't happen. Do you think we could reschedule it? I'd still like a chance to win the Great Pearl."

He laughed aloud, floated upward, and ruffled my hair. "You don't need to win the Great Pearl to prove your valor, Eliana. Not after this. But . . ."

I looked at him expectantly.

"As far as rescheduling the duels tournament." He nodded slowly. "I think that can be arranged."

Also by Catherine

Breakwater
Crosscurrent
Maelstrom

A Gathering Tempest
Daughter of the Rivers
To Wander the Paths of the Sea

Fire Dancer
Fire Mage
Fire Queen

A Note From The Author

Did you like the book? I'll be forever grateful if you take the time to leave a review on Amazon, Goodreads, or Barnes and Noble.

Reviews are the #1 way you can help other people discover the authors you love, and each and every review supports us on our journey to bring you more stories. A review doesn't have to be long or detailed—just honest! I'm so thankful for each and every one of you.

Go deep!

SPECIAL THANKS

I'm forever grateful to everyone who helped make this book possible.

Avily Jerome: Thank you for your incredible editorial comments and saving my timeline!

Jenny at Seedlings: I'm in love with the cover you designed. It's the perfect face for this story.

My Wonder Women, Lindsay, Avily, and Sarah: For your daily support in writing and life.

My writing group, Rachel and Hallie: For our Monday morning writing that helped me get over the finish line. I'm so excited to read your books!

Eliana and Nathanael: I love you! Thank you for inspiring my characters and reading my early chapters—and thanks to Eliana for reading a draft of the whole book!

About the Author

Catherine Jones Payne started writing in kindergarten and never stopped. She's the author of *Breakwater*, *Fire Dancer*, and the *Broken Tides Stories*. When she's not writing, she's probably hiking in the South Carolina mountains with her husband, contemplating her next move on a chess board, or playing with her three cats, Mildred, Minerva, and Merlin.

Made in the USA
Monee, IL
25 April 2023